剑桥双语分级阅读 · 小说馆（第2版）

原版系列编辑 Philip Prowse

In the House

屋下爱情

[英] 玛格丽特 · 约翰逊 著
徐欢欢 编译
郭建民 审订

北京语言大学出版社
BEIJING LANGUAGE AND CULTURE UNIVERSITY PRESS

CAMBRIDGE UNIVERSITY PRESS

社图号25020

北京市版权局著作权合同登记图字：01-2024-3256号

图书在版编目（CIP）数据

屋下爱情 ： 英汉对照 / （英）玛格丽特·约翰逊(Margaret Johnson) 著 ； 徐欢欢编译. -- 2版.
北京 ： 北京语言大学出版社, 2025. 3. -- (剑桥双语分级阅读小说馆). -- ISBN 978-7-5619-6739-3

Ⅰ. H319.4

中国国家版本馆CIP数据核字第2025NQ5313号

屋下爱情
WUXIA AIQING

责任编辑： 李　珍
责任印制： 周　燚

出版发行： 北京语言大学出版社
社　　址： 北京市海淀区学院路 15 号，100083
网　　址： www.blcup.com
电子信箱： service@blcup.com
电　　话： 编 辑 部 010-8230 1019
发 行 部 010-8230 3650/3591/3648
北语书店 010-8230 3653
网购咨询 010-8230 3908
印　　刷： 东港股份有限公司

版　　次：	2017 年 6 月第 1 版　2025 年 3 月第 2 版	印　　次：	2025 年 3 月第 1 次印刷
开　　本：	880 毫米 × 1230 毫米　1/32	印　　张：	6.375
字　　数：	151 千字	定　　价：	23.00 元

PRINTED IN CHINA

凡有印装质量问题，本社负责调换。售后QQ号1367565611，电话010-82303590

Preface

前言

“剑桥双语分级阅读·小说馆”是一套从剑桥大学出版社引进的面向非英语国家英语学习者的分级系列读物，由英语语言教学专家及小说作家合力创作。创作过程历时三十余年，出版后受到世界各地英语教师和英语学习者的喜爱，许多读本再版多次，三十余年来畅销不衰，成为受全球英语学习者青睐的优秀读本。

本系列读物具有以下突出特色：

1. 是原创英语读物，而非改编自普通作品的读物。因此，阅读本系列读物，我们读到的是原汁原味的原创英语，而非人为改编过的二手英语。

2. 是当代优秀短篇小说，而非年代久远的小说。因此，阅读本系列读物，我们读到的是当今鲜活的、学了就能用的英语，而非穿越时空的、学了用不上的英语；了解的是与读者同时代不同国家人们的生活和思想，而非隔代人的生活、文化和风土人情。

3. 是专为非英语国家的英语学习者量身定制的读物，而非为英语母语者所写的大众读物。因此，本系列读物是中国读者首选的英语学习读物。

4. 是英美知名小说家和英语语言教学专家合力创作的读物。小说家保障了读物的可读性与可欣赏性，英语语言教学专家保障了读物语言作为英语习得材料的科学性与可学性。本系列读物中的多个读本都曾在世界上颇具影响力的“语言学习者文学奖”（Language Learner Literature Award）评选中获得大奖。因此，阅读本系列读物，我们会在欣赏小说的同时，自然而然地、有效地提高自己的英语水平。

5. 本系列读物的故事题材丰富多样，包括侦探、情感、历险、悬疑、人文、科幻、喜剧等，读者可以随心选择自己喜欢的类别阅读；故事内容生动有趣，故事情节引人入胜、扣人心弦，读者一旦开始阅读，就想一口气读完，使阅读真正升华到“悦读”。

6. 随书附赠的音频材料内容精彩，是专业配音员的演绎再创作。听着它，我们犹如在听广播剧、听评书，又仿佛是在听电影、听话剧……这种聆听英语的享受将彻底扫除学生对英语听力的畏难心理。

7. 本系列读物所使用的语言，既有英式英语，也有美式英语，对应的音频材料也相应分为英音和美音，读者可根据自己的喜好来选择。

8. 本系列近百本读物根据《欧洲语言共同参考框架》(CEFR）和剑桥大学外语考评部开发的ESOL考试的标准来确定级别划分，是建立在科学研究和实践基础之上的分级。全套共分七个级别(与中国学生英语基础水平的大致对应关系，请参见图书封底表格)，读者可根据自己的英语基础选择相应级别的读本来学习。

为了更好地帮助中国学生学习和欣赏，“剑桥双语分级阅读·小说馆”从剑桥大学出版社原版引进后又增加了以下内容：

1. 增加了适量的辅助学习内容，包括“读前思考”“读后活动”“学习指导”三个板块，其中“学习指导”板块又包括生词、短语和表达、文化点滴、阅读练习四项内容。增加这些板块的目的是全方位帮助学生提升英语阅读能力，扩充词汇量，扫除阅读中的文化障碍，增强对英语小说的鉴赏能力。

2. 增加了小说全文的参考译文。出于语言学习的考虑，译文多采用直译，但也尽量符合中文的表达习惯。

值得一提的是，所增加的辅助学习内容和参考译文，全部由来自全国不同省市知名中学（包括人大附中、北大附中、清华附中、黄冈中学、上海中学等三十余所中学）的一线英语教师完成。这些一线教师的加盟，确保了所加内容与中国学生的英语学习特点和学习需求相吻合，为学生阅读和欣赏读物、提高英语水平给予恰到好处的助力。

英语阅读是英语课堂的延伸和补充，也是培养英语语感、提高英语水平的有效途径。选择一套好的英语读物，收获的将不仅仅是语言的进步。欢迎年轻朋友们来到“剑桥双语分级阅读·小说馆”，打开一本本好书，品味一个个好故事，为实现梦想搭建桥梁。

北京语言大学出版社

Contents 目录

People in the story

故事中的人物

Annie, Leo, Nigel, Simon, Pete: people in the *Big Eye* competition

安妮、利奥、奈杰尔、西蒙、皮特：参加《大眼》比赛的人

Big Eye: different voices who give instructions to the people in the Big Eye House

大眼：给大眼屋里的人下达指令的不同声音

Violet Carlton: a TV presenter

维奥莱特·卡尔顿：电视节目主持人

About the story

故事背景

Big Eye is a fictional reality TV programme about young people living together for forty days in the Big Eye House.

Ten young people have been chosen – out of thousands – to be on the programme and stay in the Big Eye House. They cannot see or talk to anyone outside the House and there are cameras that watch almost everything they do. People at home can watch it all on their televisions. They can also phone up to say who they want to leave the House. On Leaving Night, one person has to leave the Big Eye House and is out of the competition. The last person in the House after forty days wins a lot of money – £70,000.

《大眼》是一档虚构的电视真人秀节目，讲述的是一群年轻人在大眼屋里面一起生活四十天的故事。

从成千上万人中选出的十名年轻人来参加这个节目，并且住在大眼屋里面。他们不能与屋外的任何人见面或者交谈，而且几乎他们的一举一动都被摄像头监视着。人们在家里可以从电视上观看这一切，他们也可以给节目打电话说他们想让谁离开大眼屋。在“离别之夜”，会有一个人必须离开大眼屋并退出比赛。四十天后仍然待在这个屋子里的最后一个人将赢得一大笔钱——七万英镑。

Before reading

读前思考

1. Look at the front cover of the book. How do you think the picture relates to the title?
2. Read the blurb on the back cover. Who is the main character? Why do you think the programme is called *Big Eye*?
3. Look at the information on Page 3. How many people take part in the competition in the house? What is the aim of the competition?
4. Have you ever seen a programme like this on TV? What is your opinion of this kind of 'reality' TV programme?
5. If you have the recording, listen to Chapter 1.

Chapter 1
The carrot flower

It's not every day that you wake up to find a carrot on your bed. But that's what happened to me on Day Thirty-Six of my stay in the House.

Well, it wasn't a carrot exactly; it was a flower. A flower cut carefully out of a carrot with a knife. I know it sounds a bit odd, but it was really beautiful, honestly. I felt pleased that somebody had taken the trouble to make it for me. But I had no idea who that 'somebody' might be. I knew who I *wanted* it to be though – Simon. Simon had beautiful hands, along with a beautiful body and a handsome face. But were they hands that could make such a flower? I hoped so.

Looking around the bedroom, I saw that Leo was still in bed. There was one bedroom for all of us in the House with ten beds in it. But no-one was using five of the beds any more, since five people had already left the House. I looked at Leo sleeping. Big Eye turns the lights on in the bedroom at eight o'clock every morning, but that doesn't wake Leo up. Nothing wakes

Leo up until he wants to wake up. So he can't have made the flower, I thought. It wasn't the kind of thing he'd do anyway. Leo prefers talking to doing.

Suddenly a voice filled the room. 'This is Big Eye. Would Annie come to the Diary Room please?'

The Diary Room was the place we went to for private conversations with Big Eye. Well, they were private because the other people in the House couldn't hear what you said. But actually they were very public, because everyone watching the *Big Eye* programme on TV could see and hear you. But you usually forgot about that.

Putting on my dressing gown, I put the carrot flower carefully in my pocket. For some reason I wanted to keep it a secret, although I knew this was silly. Thousands, or maybe even millions, of television viewers had already seen me find it.

'Morning, guys.' Out in the main living area, Pete and Nigel were making breakfast. They smiled at me.

'Morning, Annie.'

I looked at both of them as I walked towards the Diary Room. Nigel was a very intelligent man, but he wasn't very good with his hands. I couldn't imagine him being able to make my carrot flower. Pete was an engineer though. Maybe it was him?

I looked out of the window, searching for Simon. There he was, jogging as usual. Every morning, he ran for an hour before breakfast. He'd already worn out some of the grass in the small garden. By the time the competition ended on Saturday there probably wouldn't be any grass left at all. Had Simon taken some time off from his exercise to make my presents? It would be very nice if he had – very nice indeed.

Smiling to myself, I pressed the button on the wall outside the Diary Room door. As I waited for the door to open, I continued watching Simon. If the women watching the programme were anything like me, then Simon and his beautiful body had an excellent chance of winning this competition. The winner would be the person who managed to stay in the House the longest. And the prize for the winner was £70,000. Now there were only four days left until the competition was over.

On Leaving Night thousands of people phoned the TV station to vote – to say which person they wanted to leave the House. At first, Leaving Nights had taken place once a week, on Saturdays. And five people had left the Big Eye House. But now the competition was almost over, there were going to be two extra Leaving

Nights. By Saturday, the last day of the competition, there would only be three people left.

Leaving Nights were always the same. Everyone in the House had to sit on the sofas and wait for Violet Carlton, the TV presenter, to tell us who was leaving. So far Simon had always been safe – he hadn't got many votes at all. Neither had I actually. Very few people had phoned to say either of us should leave. I don't know why I was popular. I'm not ugly, but I'm certainly not beautiful.

I was still staring at Simon when I heard the door to the Diary Room start to open. I began to walk into the room. I didn't realise that the door wasn't open wide enough for me to be able to go in. My arm hit the door.

'Ow!' I said, holding my hurt arm. Pete and Nigel looked over.

'OK, Annie?' Pete asked.

'Yes,' I said. 'Just another injury.' All the men were used to me having accidents. I was always dropping something or falling over something.

I was still holding my arm as I sat down on the chair in the Diary Room. Or rather, *in* the chair, because it's so big and so soft you have to half-lie on it.

It's impossible to sit in it without relaxing. I think Big Eye knows we'll be more open about what we say if we're relaxed.

'Good morning, Annie,' said Big Eye.

I was halfway through a yawn. 'Good morning, Big Eye,' I said, smiling at the camera in front of me. Big Eye had four or five different voices, depending on what time it was. Sometimes Big Eye was a *he*, and sometimes Big Eye was a *she*. This morning it was the man with the soft voice, a voice like milk chocolate. I liked him.

'And how are you feeling this morning, Annie?' Big Eye asked.

'Fine,' I said, still smiling. 'Very good, in fact.'

'Is there any special reason why you're feeling so good this morning, Annie?'

I could feel the carrot flower under my fingers in my pocket. I knew Big Eye wanted me to talk about it, but I still wanted to keep it to myself. 'Well, things are quite peaceful in here at the moment, I suppose,' I said.

'And why do you think that is, Annie?' asked Big Eye.

I thought about it. 'I suppose it's because Janine and Gloria have gone,' I said. 'They made a lot of trouble, those two.'

Janine and Gloria had both been very loud people. *Obvious* people. As well as the prize money for the winner, there was £10,000 for anyone who had a romance in the House. Both Janine and Gloria had tried very hard to have a romance with Simon.

'Is there any other reason why you feel so good this morning, Annie?' asked Big Eye.

I looked at the camera. It seemed as if Big Eye wasn't going to give up. 'Yes,' I said at last. 'You know there is. Somebody left me a present again. Yesterday it was that beautiful paper boat, and today it was ... this.' I brought the carrot flower out of my pocket and held it in my hand in front of the camera. 'It's lovely, isn't it?'

Big Eye didn't give an opinion. Big Eye *never* gave opinions. 'Do you know who gave you this present, Annie?'

I shook my head. 'No, I don't. It's a complete mystery. I tried to find out who made me the paper boat yesterday, and nobody would admit to it. So I don't know who my secret present-giver is.' Then I realised something, and looked at the camera, wide-eyed. 'But *you* know, don't you? You must do. You know what's going on all over the House.'

The Big Eye House has cameras everywhere, except for inside the shower and the toilets. The cameras can even see us at night – there are special cameras that work in the dark.

'Who is it?' I asked Big Eye. 'Who's been leaving me these presents?'

'Big Eye cannot give you that information, Annie,' Big Eye said.

'You mean you don't *want* to,' I said.

Big Eye stayed silent. I put the carrot flower back into my pocket, suddenly realising (I'm a bit slow in the mornings before I've had a cup of strong coffee) that if Big Eye knew who was giving me the presents, then everybody knew. That was, everybody in the United Kingdom who was watching the *Big Eye* programme. It was very strange to think that millions of people knew more about what was happening to me than I did myself.

'How does it feel to be the only woman left in the House, Annie?' Big Eye asked.

I thought about it. 'Well, I suppose I'm not sure what the men really think of me any more. I mean, they're being very nice to me, but how do I know if they really like me or not? Maybe they're just being nice to me because they want to start a romance and win £10,000.'

'And how do you feel about having a romance with someone in the House?' Big Eye asked next.

I immediately thought about Simon and smiled to myself. 'I'm not sure,' I said to Big Eye. 'The men left are all very different, aren't they? I like some things about all of them.'

There was a pause. Big Eye often leaves pauses. He wants you to feel uncomfortable so you say anything just to fill the silence. I don't mind silence myself. I think that comes from working in a museum. Museums can be quite silent places, especially in the summer. People don't want to look at old pictures and furniture when the sun is out.

'Big Eye has some instructions for you now, Annie,' Big Eye said.

'Oh?' I said and waited.

'You are to tell Leo, Simon, Pete and Nigel that Big Eye wishes them to write a poem for you. This poem should say how they feel about you.'

'A poem?' I said, feeling suddenly annoyed that I only had a camera to look at. I wanted to be able to stare Mr Milk Chocolate right in the face. 'You mean like:

Roses are red,
Violets are blue,
Sugar is sweet
And so are you?'

'Everyone is allowed to decide what type of poem they want to write themselves,' Big Eye said.

'They'll hate it!' I said, not looking forward to going out there and telling them all.

Big Eye continued, obviously not worried about how the men might feel. 'They must complete their poems by ten-thirty this morning,' he said. 'At eleven o'clock you will read the poems out and decide which poem is the best. The poems should be anonymous – nobody should sign their poem and you should not know who has written them. This is the task for today.'

Every day we were given something to do – a task. This was partly to keep us busy, but mostly to interest the viewers at home. Some people enjoyed just watching us cleaning the House or chatting to each other by the pool in the garden. I have no idea why. But most people wanted to see us doing silly things. While I'd been in the House I'd dressed up as a horse with

Simon, taken part in a singing competition (I came last), and had a girls against boys water fight in the garden (the boys won). We had to do what Big Eye told us – those were the rules of the Big Eye competition.

'Big Eye would like you to go and tell the others about today's task now, Annie,' Big Eye told me. I pushed myself out of the chair.

'OK then,' I said. 'Bye for now.'

'Goodbye, Annie,' Big Eye said.

I left the Diary Room to go and break the bad news to the guys.

Chapter 2
As blue as the sea

It's difficult to describe what it was like, living in the House. You didn't exactly forget your life outside – your friends, your family, your job – but they almost felt like a story you'd heard. The House was the reality – with its rooms, people, and Big Eye telling us what to do.

You even forgot about the cameras most of the time. I know that probably sounds unbelievable, but you did. There were so many of them everywhere, recording every little thing we did or said. But you got so used to it; you stopped thinking about it. We were like fish swimming around in a bowl, except it was a bowl we couldn't see out of. We didn't know what was happening in the world outside. The House, and what happened in it, was our world. Which is why something like a stupid competition to write a poem became so important.

When I broke the news about the task, none of the guys seemed very happy about it, but Nigel was especially annoyed. 'That's not fair!' he complained, after I'd described what Big Eye wanted them to do. 'I don't even like writing shopping lists! I wouldn't even know how to *begin* to write a poem. And *he's* a writer already.' Nigel pointed at Leo, who had climbed out of bed five minutes before, when Big Eye had ordered everybody to meet on the sofas. He was holding onto the mug of coffee Pete had made him as if it were life-saving medicine.

'I write detective stories, not poems,' he said with a yawn. 'And anyway, I have to be really interested in something to want to write.'

'You mean you have to be inspired?' Pete asked.

Leo nodded, drinking some of his coffee. 'That's right. I have to be inspired.'

'And you feel more inspired by a dead body than by Annie?' asked Simon, looking over at me. 'That's not very nice, is it, Annie?'

Leo smiled at me. 'Sorry, Annie, I'm afraid it's true. Blood, fear and mystery – that's what I'm inspired by.'

I felt annoyed, but tried not to show it. Out of all the men in the House, Leo was the one who had made the least effort to get me to like him. He was the same with everybody though – Leo was just Leo, and we could take him or leave him. But somehow we liked him anyway. He was very sociable, and even though he could be lazy, he was also funny and interesting. I didn't think Leo had ever had to try very hard with people.

'Well,' I said, 'I hope you're all going to co-operate. You've all got to do the task, so there's no point in complaining. You know what will happen if you don't.'

'No nice food,' Nigel said.

Big Eye gave us the very basic food we needed, like bread, rice and potatoes, but we had to earn anything more than that by doing these tasks successfully.

'And it's Tuesday today,' Nigel went on.

'Takeaway night!' said Pete.

On Tuesdays, if we'd achieved our task, Big Eye gave us beer and a takeaway meal from an Indian or a Chinese restaurant. We all enjoyed takeaway night. Even Simon, who usually only ate healthy food.

'We'd better get busy then!' said Leo, and he went back towards the bedroom, taking his cup of coffee with him.

'Don't forget – no names on the poems. They must be anonymous,' I called after him.

The others went out into the garden. When I tried to follow them, Simon told me to stay indoors. 'I won't be able to think properly if you're around,' he said. 'I'll feel too stupid.'

'Me too,' agreed Pete. 'Sorry, Annie.'

'That's OK,' I said. 'I'll do a bit of cleaning. This place is a mess.'

It was true. Janine had been the one who liked cleaning. When she hadn't been trying to get Simon alone, she had been busy with the hoover or washing the kitchen floor. It had been a bit annoying at the time – you couldn't put your coffee cup down for a moment without Janine taking it away to wash it up. But now she wasn't with us any more and the place was getting dirty, I missed her. Well, to be honest, I missed the work she had done, not her. She hadn't been very nice to me at all.

As I got the hoover out and got started, I was still thinking about how the guys had taken the news about the task. None of them had wanted to do it. While I knew it wasn't easy to write poems, I did feel they might at least have pretended that I was a good subject for a poem. But as it was, they had all complained about it. Leo had even said he would rather write about dead bodies. None of which was very good for a girl's confidence.

I was so busy feeling sorry for myself as I worked that I didn't notice what was happening. The hoover had 'eaten' the edge of the carpet and was beginning to make a very strange noise.

'Oh no!' I said worriedly, trying to pull the hoover away, but it wouldn't come free. The edge of the carpet was stuck inside the hoover. The noise was deafening – the hoover sounded as if it was going to explode. I bent over to try to pull the carpet free, but I couldn't. Then suddenly the hoover stopped screaming.

I looked round. Leo had turned the hoover off at the plug in the wall and was standing laughing at me. 'I know I said I was inspired by murder, Annie,' he said, 'but what has that carpet ever done to you?'

I looked at him, speaking crossly because I was embarrassed. 'Shouldn't you be writing your poem?' I asked.

Leo walked over to the kettle and turned it on. 'Finished it,' he said.

I stood up, leaving the hoover where it was. I'd had quite enough of cleaning for one morning. 'That was a bit quick,' I said.

Leo just smiled. 'Do you want a coffee?' he asked.

Suddenly a coffee was the thing I wanted more than

anything else in the world. What had I been thinking of, trying to do the cleaning without a cup of coffee inside me first? No wonder it had all gone wrong. 'Oh yes, please!' I said.

But Leo had left the kettle and gone over to the sofa to sit down. 'Two sugars in mine,' he said. 'And not too much milk.'

'Leo!' I said. 'I thought you were offering to make *me* a cup of coffee!'

He laughed. 'I know,' he said.

That was just like Leo. I don't know how he did it. If any of the other guys had tried such a joke on me I'd have felt really cross. But somehow I found myself laughing with Leo and going off to make the coffee. If anybody got away with murder, it was Leo.

'There you are,' I said, coming back with the coffee. 'You're lucky I'm not throwing it at you.'

Leo smiled and took his coffee. 'I *am*, aren't I?' he said. 'With all the accidents you have. How do you manage to do your job?'

'What do you mean?' I asked.

'Well,' he said, 'museums are full of valuable stuff, right? And you have accidents all the time. Don't you keep on breaking things?'

I *had* broken a very old plate once, but I wasn't going to tell Leo and everyone watching the programme about that. My boss still hadn't forgotten about it, and neither had I. 'I don't get to touch the things in the museum very often,' I told Leo. 'My job is to introduce the museum to groups of schoolchildren who visit for the day.'

Leo laughed. 'You mean you say, "Museum, this is Mary, Ellen and Peter from Foxwood School"?' he joked.

'No,' I said patiently. 'I mean I organise activities for the children to do – drawing or painting activities inspired by things in the museum, or questions for them to answer as they go round.'

It wasn't the job I had always wanted, if I was honest. It was usually OK – if you didn't get a group of badly behaved boys running about or hiding somewhere. But it wasn't what I'd hoped to do after I'd left university.

'If you could do anything in the world, what would you do?' asked Leo, and I answered him straight away. I didn't need to think about it.

'I'd travel abroad photographing and writing about beautiful things and places,' I said.

'Are you good at photography?' Leo asked.

'No,' I said, 'not at the moment.'

Leo laughed.

'But I can learn,' I told him.

'This is Big Eye,' Big Eye interrupted us. 'All poems must be completed by ten-thirty. Would Leo please come to the Diary Room?'

Leo looked up towards the ceiling, where the voice seemed to come from. 'Do I have to?' he asked, but Big Eye made no reply. 'I'll take that as a "yes" then,' Leo said, getting up with a sigh.

He was back quickly, carrying lots of clothes in his arms. 'Big Eye wanted me to collect this lot,' he said.

'What is it?' I asked, surprised.

'The clothes we've all got to wear while you read out our poems. Big Eye obviously wants us to look smart.'

I went over to take a look. There were four black suits and a beautiful long dress made out of shiny green material. I touched it. 'How lovely!' I said.

'Lovely for you!' Leo said unhappily. 'I only wear a suit to weddings!'

By eleven o'clock, the men were all dressed in their suits, and I was wearing the long green dress. I had put my hair up too, and I felt good.

'You look lovely, Annie,' Pete said. 'That colour really suits you.'

I smiled at him, thinking what a nice man he was. I'd never heard him say anything unpleasant about anyone, and he was always so helpful. 'Thank you, Pete,' I said. 'And so do you. You *all* do.' It was true – they did. The suits made them all look handsome and ... well, more adult, I suppose.

'This is Big Eye,' Big Eye said. 'The poetry competition will begin in two minutes. Please put all poems in the box on the table. You are reminded that the poems should be anonymous – your name should *not* appear on your poem.'

'Perhaps you should look away, Annie,' Nigel suggested, 'so you don't see us putting our poems into the box.' Nigel always liked to do things properly. He would never break any of Big Eye's rules.

'OK,' I said. 'Good idea.' And I turned away.

'They're all in,' Pete told me after a moment, and I turned back.

'This is Big Eye. The competition will now begin. Annie, please begin reading.'

I stood up and went over to the box. I put my hand inside and pulled out a piece of paper. The writing on it was small and very tidy. I began to read.

'Annie's eyes are as blue as the sea ...' I read. Leo laughed loudly and I came to a stop. I looked at him crossly. 'No laughing,' I said, 'or I won't be able to do it.'

'Yes,' said Pete. 'Remember takeaway night!'

'Sorry,' said Leo, still smiling. 'I'll do my best not to laugh.'

Nigel's face was bright red. I thought I knew why – he was the sort of man to have small, tidy writing. I guessed it was his poem.

'I'll begin again,' I said, and gave a little cough to clear my throat.

'Annie's eyes are as blue as the sea;
They make me hope she'll go out with me.
I haven't asked her yet, so until that day,
I hope she'll come to like me in every way.
I want to help her learn to cook,
I want to teach her to enjoy a good book.
We're very different, but here's the thing,
I really want her to wear my ring.'

Leo's shoulders had started to shake halfway through the poem. He had his hand over his mouth, but I could see tears of laughter running down his face. Pete and Simon were smiling too, but Nigel looked completely embarrassed.

'That was, er ... very nice,' I said, not sure what else to say. At that, Leo couldn't hide his laughter any longer. It exploded out loudly, and Nigel got angrily to his feet.

'Oh, grow up, Leo!' he shouted.

Chapter 3
Winners and jokes

Leo tried to stop laughing, but didn't manage it.

'It was a very ... nice poem,' I said again, though I hadn't actually liked it at all. The writer, Nigel, didn't seem to be happy with me. He'd wanted to change a lot about me, but he still said he wanted me to wear his ring. I found *that* rather hard to believe.

Nigel was still staring angrily at Leo. 'You never take anything seriously, do you, Leo?' he said.

Leo smiled. 'I try not to,' he said.

'Come on, Nigel,' Pete said gently. 'Sit down, eh? This is only supposed to be a bit of fun.'

Nigel sat down and Pete looked over at me. 'Maybe you ought to move on to the next poem, Annie,' he suggested.

That seemed like a good idea. 'OK,' I said. 'Poem number two.' I gave another little cough before I began.

'She's like a sleepy mouse when she wakes up,
Until she's drunk from her coffee cup.

She has accidents every day,
Falling over things that are in the way.
She uses the wrong words and she drops the tea,
But this crazy girl is the one for me.'

This poem made nearly everyone smile. Even I thought it was quite sweet, and a lot like me. From the look on his face, I thought Pete had written it.

'OK,' I said, taking another piece of paper out of the box. 'Poem number three.' The writing was confident and angry-looking. Without reading a word, I guessed the poem was Simon's.

'Not sporty,
Not forty.
Not too fat,
Thanks for that!
A bad cook,
With a good look.
She's very funny,
Even without the money.
But as it's there,
Why not share?
Ann, Ann, Ann;
I'm your man!'

Leo was laughing again. I didn't want to look at

Simon, because I was sure he would have a face like murder, so I moved quickly on.

'Right,' I said. 'The last poem – poem number four.' It was the shortest of all of them.

'She's not boring, she's good fun;
Annie is twenty different women in one.
Likes to laugh, makes mistakes,
Always burns her chocolate cakes!'

We all laughed at that one. The week before it had been Pete's birthday and I'd decided to make him a birthday cake. Unfortunately, I'd forgotten all about it after I'd put it in the oven. It had been a lovely hot day, and we'd all been outside in the pool. None of us had smelt the cake until it was completely black and burnt.

'This is Big Eye. All the poems have been read. Annie should now decide which poem is the best. The prize for the winner will be a date with Annie.'

'That's great!' somebody said – Simon, I think. I wasn't sure because I was busy trying to decide who I wanted to win. I was supposed to decide which poem was best, but it was difficult to keep to that rule. I thought I knew who had written each poem, and the prize was a date with me. I'm only human, after all, so I was trying to decide who I wanted to have a date with.

Not Nigel; I'd gone off him with all his talk about rings and helping me to read books. Didn't he think I had to read books for my job? And as for cooking, *he* wasn't exactly an amazing cook himself. The curry he'd made the other night had been almost too hot to eat. No, not Nigel, which meant not poem number one.

Leo? No, that would be like having a date with my brother. His poem was obviously poem number four, as it was the shortest and Leo had been so quick writing it.

Pete then; poem number two? Well, Pete was nice. My mum would want me to choose Pete, and I *did* like him. But really, there was only one choice – Simon, with his film-star good looks. An evening of him smiling at me across a table would be very enjoyable. So, poem number three it was.

'Will Annie please name the winning poem,' Big Eye ordered me, and I took a deep breath.

'The winner of the poetry competition is ...' I paused, looking at each of the men in turn. Leo had his usual smile on his face, but the others looked as if they cared about the result. I suddenly felt very powerful. 'Poem number three!'

'Yes!' Leo said, throwing his arms into the air.

'What?' I said.

'I told you!' Nigel said angrily, standing up. 'I told you he would win. He's a *writer*! It was always going to be him!'

'For once I agree with you, Nigel,' Simon said, not looking happy. 'The whole competition was a complete waste of time.'

I was confused. I looked at Leo. '*You* wrote poem number three?' I asked, and he nodded.

'I certainly did!' he said, smiling all over his face.

'Well done, Leo,' Pete said, ever the nice guy.

'Leo,' said Big Eye, 'your prize is a date with Annie this evening. You should both go to the Diary Room at eight o'clock. Everyone else should know that no takeaway meal will be provided for them this evening.'

Simon was still looking fed up. 'Do you know what?' he said. 'I'm going to the Diary Room to tell Big Eye exactly what I think about this. It isn't fair.' And off he went.

'And I'm going to have a short sleep,' said Leo, getting up with a yawn. 'Writing poetry makes me very tired.'

'Take your suit off,' Pete advised him. 'You'll need to look smart for your big date tonight.'

Leo nodded and gave me a big smile. 'Can't wait,' he said, and then he went to the bedroom, leaving me with Pete and Nigel.

'Well,' said Pete, 'I think I'd better not give up my engineering job. I'm obviously not a good poet!'

I looked at him. 'They were *all* good,' I said, still feeling disappointed that I wasn't going to be having a date with Simon. Especially as he was so disappointed about losing. He had obviously *wanted* to win a date with me.

Pete laughed. 'I think you ought to read more poetry, Annie, if you think that! Anyone for a cup of tea?'

'All right,' said Nigel sadly. 'I suppose I may as well.'

'Annie?' asked Pete.

I shook my head. 'No thanks, Pete,' I said, still thinking about the competition. I'd been so sure that Simon had written poem number three. I looked through the poems, pulling out poem number three and reading some of it again.

She's very funny, even without the money. But as it's there, why not share? What did Leo mean by that? Was he suggesting we had a romance to win the £10,000? Well, if he was, then he was going to be out of luck!

'Er ... did you like my poem, Annie?' Nigel asked.

I looked up at him. 'Which poem was yours?' I asked, even though I knew.

'Poem number one,' he said. 'I was quite pleased with it myself.' And as he smiled, he *did* look very pleased with himself indeed.

Suddenly I felt extremely angry with him. While I wasn't prepared to pretend to have a romance to win some money, I *was* prepared to make fun of Nigel. Well, it was only fair – he shouldn't have written all that rubbish in his poem.

I put the poems down and went to sit next to him. 'Oh yes, Nigel,' I said softly, looking right into his eyes. 'I *loved* your poem! How *kind* of you to want to help me learn new things!'

Nigel's smile grew. 'I thought you'd like that bit,' he said, not realising at all that I was getting more and more cross with him.

'But,' I said, moving closer and putting my hand on his arm, 'the bit I *really* liked the best was the bit where you said you wanted me to wear your ring!'

'Oh, that bit,' said Nigel, starting to look a bit doubtful.

'Yes!' I said, still staring into his eyes. 'I *loved* that bit. And ... the answer's yes!'

Nigel's face was looking a bit white now. He tried to move away from me, but I pulled his arm to bring him closer again. 'What ... what do you mean?' he asked in a whisper.

'Well,' I explained, 'in that poem you asked me to marry you, didn't you? And the answer's yes!'

I'd never seen a man look so frightened before. His eyes were huge. It was *so* funny. I might just have managed not to explode with laughter though, if Pete hadn't started laughing.

'Can't you see she's joking, Nigel?' he said, coming back with the tea.

And then I let go of Nigel's arm and laughed so much my stomach hurt. 'You looked so worried!' I said to him when I could finally speak again.

Nigel looked at me crossly. 'That's not funny,' he said.

'Oh yes, it is,' Pete said, and that started me off laughing all over again.

'You shouldn't have put it in your poem if you didn't mean it,' I told him after a while.

'I couldn't think of anything else,' Nigel said crossly.

Simon came out of the Diary Room. He looked even more fed up than ever. 'I tried to tell them it wasn't a fair competition,' he told us, 'but they wouldn't say anything.'

'What about the takeaway?' Nigel wanted to know.

Simon shook his head. 'They wouldn't change their minds about that either. No takeaway.'

'Never mind,' Pete said. 'How about a nice cup of tea?'

Simon looked angry. 'That's your answer to everything, isn't it?' he said. 'A nice cup of tea. No thanks.' And with that, he went out into the garden, closing the door noisily after him.

'Now that is one disappointed man,' Pete said, as we all sat and stared after Simon.

Nigel was still cross with me. 'He's disappointed about the takeaway, *not* losing out on a date with Annie,' he said.

'Thanks, Nigel,' I said, getting up and following Simon.

He was sitting on the garden seat. His sunglasses hid his eyes, but his mouth showed how fed up he was. I sat next to him without saying anything for a moment.

Then I said, 'I'm sorry about the takeaway.'

He tried to smile. 'I'm not worried about the takeaway,' he said. 'I'm just a bit fed up with being stuck in here.'

'Are you?' I asked.

'Yes,' he said. 'It's not how I imagined it would be. All the sitting around with nothing to do; all the stupid chat. Sometimes it's like an old people's home in here! I've never been so bored in all my life.'

'Oh,' I said, disappointed that Simon felt that way.

'Look, you're all nice people; it's not that,' Simon went on. 'Especially you, Annie. It's just that I'm the type of person who needs goals to work towards, and I'm not talking about silly music shows or poetry competitions. Maybe it would be best if I was the one to leave next.'

'Well,' I said, my face going red as I spoke, 'I don't want you to leave.'

Simon smiled at me. I wished he wasn't wearing the sunglasses so I could see his eyes.

'It *would* be boring in here without you,' I went on.

Simon took my hand. I felt the electricity from his touch go right up my arm. 'You're very sweet, Annie,' he said. 'Don't listen to me. I'm just feeling sorry for myself.'

He was still holding my hand, and it made me feel brave. 'I'm sorry you didn't win the competition,' I told him. 'I ... I wanted you to win.'

'Ah,' Simon said, 'poor Annie. Are you very disappointed your date isn't with me?'

My face was turning even redder. 'Yes, I am,' I said. 'Are ... are you?'

Simon's white-toothed smile shone out again. '*Of course* I am,' he said. With his free hand he reached out to touch my hair. His fingers were long and confident. Perfect for making carrot flowers and paper boats. 'Look at you,' he said.

'What?' I asked, putting a hand up to my hair. It wasn't all on top of my head any more – most of it had dropped down around my shoulders. I must look a real mess. If only I had my comb.

'Funny, messy Annie,' Simon said softly. 'How nice it would be to have a date with you! But we'll just have to do something special together another time, won't we?'

Soon after that Simon decided he was going to do some more jogging. I watched him for a while, and then I walked dreamily back indoors. Maybe there would be a romance in the House after all – a romance between Simon and me!

Chapter 4

Messy spaghetti

At exactly eight o'clock, Leo and I went to the Diary Room together. Leo was still wearing his suit, and he still looked smart. Well, almost smart – his tie wasn't quite straight. As for me, I'm afraid I didn't look quite as smart as I had in the morning. At lunchtime we'd had soup and some had got on my dress. Although I'd done my best to clean it off, you could still see where it had been. Soup and I just didn't go together. I wished I'd changed out of the dress.

'Do you think we're going to have our date in the Diary Room?' Leo asked, and I looked at him, surprised.

'No!' I said, but actually I hadn't thought about it. 'You don't think so, do you?'

'Well,' said Leo, 'dates are supposed to be private, aren't they? And the Diary Room, the toilets and the shower are the only private places, aren't they?' He smiled down at me. 'Got your soap?'

'Good evening, Annie. Good evening, Leo,' said Big Eye. It was a woman this time.

'Hi there, Big Eye,' said Leo.

'Hello, Big Eye,' I said, and for some strange reason I suddenly felt a bit nervous. I couldn't imagine why – this was only Leo, after all. Now, if it had been *Simon* I was waiting to have a date with, *then* I would have had a good reason to feel nervous.

'Your date this evening will be a meal for two,' Big Eye told us. I half-expected Leo to make a joke about eating dinner in the shower, but he didn't.

'If you press the button on the wall behind the chair, a door will open,' Big Eye told us. 'Go through, and you will find your table waiting for you.'

Leo and I looked at each other, smiling. A secret door – how exciting!

'Thank you, Big Eye,' I said.

Leo was already reaching behind the chair.

'Got it!' he said, and next moment the wall was opening up and he was walking through to the room on the other side. 'Come on, Annie!' he said, and I quickly followed him. It felt like a real adventure.

'Oh!' I said as I got inside. *'Oh!'*

The room was beautiful. It was small, and it was painted a pinkish red colour. The table was covered in a beautiful tablecloth made of shiny red material, and it was laid with shining silver knives and forks. But it was the lights that took my breath away as I went in. They were everywhere you looked - tiny silver-white lights that made the room look warm. It was extremely romantic.

Leo was holding out one of the chairs for me. 'Do sit down,' he said with a smile.

I laughed. 'Thank you, kind sir,' I said.

Leo went round to the other side of the table and sat down himself. As he did, the secret door closed.

'We're shut in,' I said.

Leo looked up at the cameras on the wall. 'Just you, me and a million or two viewers then,' he joked.

'I wonder how we're going to get our food?' I asked.

'Good question,' said Leo, but at that moment Big Eye spoke.

'Welcome to the Big Eye Restaurant,' she said.

I caught Leo's eye - he had a big smile on his face - and I had to put a hand over my mouth to stop myself from laughing.

'Your first course is ready,' Big Eye told us. 'Press the button under the table and a door will open.'

'They like their buttons here, don't they?' Leo said, bending down to have a look.

'Let me press it this time!' I said, and quickly bent down to look under the table. 'Where is it?' And I began feeling around under the table. It was difficult to see, because I had the tablecloth in my eyes. I pushed it out of the way and saw Leo smiling at me under the table.

'You look different upside down,' he said.

'You don't,' I laughed. 'You look about the same.'

'Thanks!' he said. 'And the button's there, I think.'

I saw where he was pointing. 'Oh yes,' I said, and reached out to press it. Immediately there was a noise from somewhere above, and I quickly moved my head to see what was happening. Unfortunately I moved a bit too quickly and managed to hit my head on the table.

'Ow!' I said, holding my head.

'Are you OK?' asked Leo.

'Yes, yes,' I said impatiently. 'Look over there!'

A small door had opened, showing a hole in the wall. In it were two bowls.

'Allow me,' said Leo, who was clearly on his best behaviour this evening. He went over to the hole in the wall and came back with two bowls of delicious-looking fruit.

'I'm pleased it isn't soup,' I said.

Leo smiled. 'Big Eye wouldn't be that horrible to you twice in a day,' he said.

'Wouldn't he?' I said, picking up a piece of fruit.

'She, tonight,' Leo said.

'Oh yes,' I said. 'Sorry, she. What *is* this fruit?' I asked. 'Do you know?'

'No idea,' Leo said. 'Something unusual. It smells nice though.'

I put the fruit in my mouth and took a bite. Immediately juice from the fruit ran right down my arm. 'Oh!' I said, and Leo laughed. 'Why didn't that happen to you?' I asked.

He shook his head. 'I don't know, Annie,' he said. 'It's one of the unexplained facts of life. Annie Tyler equals mess and accidents.'

'I'm not completely hopeless,' I said, trying to get the juice off my arm with a handkerchief and starting to feel a bit annoyed.

'Of course not,' Leo agreed. 'You're not sporty, not forty. Not too fat ...'

'OK, OK,' I interrupted him. 'Thank you. Anyway, what does Leo Brown equal? If I'm mess and accidents, what are you?'

'You tell me,' Leo said, taking a large bite of his fruit. 'What do you think Leo Brown equals?'

'Joking and sleeping,' I said, without having to think

about it. 'Leo Brown equals joking and sleeping.'

'That's in *here*,' Leo told me. 'But that's not the real Leo Brown.'

'So what is the "real" Leo Brown like?' I asked, attempting another bite of fruit.

'Well, he thinks a lot, and after he's thought, he actually works very hard. When he's not meeting up with his friends and being sociable.'

'You think a lot here too,' I told him.

'Do I?' asked Leo.

I nodded. 'Yes. Oh, you chat and you make your jokes, but you watch us too. And you listen to what we say very carefully. Sometimes I think we'll all end up as characters in one of your books.'

Leo shook his head. 'Before I came to the Big Eye House, I had to promise that I wouldn't use anything that happens here in my future writing. That includes any of the people I meet in here. So don't worry; you're safe. You won't pick up one of my books in an airport and discover I've made you a murderer in it.'

'I wouldn't be a very believable murderer anyway,' I told him. 'Not with all the mistakes I make.'

'What's the worst mistake you've ever made?' Leo asked. 'Your most embarrassing moment.'

I thought about it. There were so many to choose from. 'Well,' I said, 'there was the time when my bikini top fell off when I jumped into the swimming pool. And the time I was working in a hospital when I was a student. I had to give patients their meals in their beds and I dropped a big bowl of peas on the floor. They went under everyone's beds.'

Leo began to laugh. I didn't mind; it *was* funny now, looking back on it. It had taken ages to find all the peas.

'And it wasn't a very good moment when I locked two schoolboys in one of the rooms in the museum,' I continued.

'Did you *intend* to lock them in?' Leo asked.

'No!' I said impatiently. 'Of course I didn't. I had no idea they were in there. They were hiding from their teacher for a joke. I thought everyone had come out of the room, so I locked up. It's a room that people can only go into with someone from the museum.'

'Were they in there all night?' Leo wanted to know.

'No,' I said. 'Only ten minutes or so. But I had turned the lights off, so it was quite dark, and there were some Egyptian bodies in there – you know, mummies.'

Leo laughed. 'I imagine those boys will never run off to hide again,' he said.

'They may never even visit a museum again,' I said. 'They were really afraid. And the teacher was very angry about it. I got into big trouble with my boss.'

'Poor Annie,' Leo said.

'I do get tired of people thinking I'm hopeless all the time.' I said. 'It would be nice to be taken seriously.'

Leo looked at me. 'You have fruit juice on the end of your nose,' he said.

I reached crossly for my – now very wet – handkerchief. 'You see?' I said, using it on my nose. 'There's absolutely no hope of anyone ever taking me seriously, is there?'

There was a sound at the hole in the wall. Leo and I both looked up at the same time and saw – two large plates of very messy spaghetti bolognese.

'Oh, no!' I said. 'I'm useless at eating spaghetti!' Then I looked at Leo and we both began to laugh.

'OK,' he said, collecting up our fruit bowls. 'I've got a suggestion.'

'What?' I asked.

'Well,' Leo said, going over to collect the spaghetti,

'Big Eye has obviously given us spaghetti to eat for a reason.'

'Yes,' I said, 'to make me look as stupid as possible!'

'My suggestion is that we *both* look stupid. We both make as much mess as possible. We don't even try to keep our clothes clean. If Big Eye wants mess, let's give her mess!'

I smiled at him. 'You're crazy,' I told him. 'Do you know that?'

'Plenty of past girlfriends have told me so,' he said. He put one of the plates of spaghetti on the table in front of me. 'But I also like to think I'm fun. So what do you say? Shall we have a bit of messy fun?'

It was going to happen anyway with me eating spaghetti. It might as well be planned. 'OK then,' I said. 'Let's do it!'

'Right,' said Leo, lifting his fork. 'One, two, three, go!'

Chapter 5 Leaving Night

By the end of our meal, my face was red with bolognese sauce and Leo had spaghetti in his hair. There was spaghetti everywhere and we had laughed so much I was exhausted. It was like being five years old all over again.

I smiled at Leo across the table. 'Thanks,' I said.

'What for?' he asked.

'Well,' I said, 'for making this fun. It would have been awful to eat that meal with someone who was embarrassed about me making a mess.'

Leo looked at me. 'And which of the other guys would have been embarrassed, do you think?'

I thought about it. 'Nigel, probably. Yes, definitely Nigel. He would have been so embarrassed about it, the whole meal would have been silent.'

'Except for the sound of you eating spaghetti?' Leo smiled.

'Yes,' I agreed, 'except for that.'

'Who else would have been embarrassed, do you think?'

I thought about it again. 'Pete, probably,' I said. 'But he would be far too nice to mention it.'

'Pleasant Pete,' Leo said, and I smiled.

'He *is* Pleasant Pete,' I said.

Leo looked at me. 'What about Simon?' he asked. 'If Pete is Pleasant Pete, what's Simon?'

I played with the spaghetti I had left on my plate with my fork. *Sexy* Simon, I thought, but I didn't say that. 'Sporty Simon?' I suggested instead.

'And me?' Leo asked.

I looked at him, giving it some thought. 'Laughing Leo,' I said. 'Definitely. And sometimes – especially when we need someone to wash up the dirty plates – Lazy Leo.'

Leo smiled at me. 'Don't be Awful Annie,' he joked, and I laughed.

'Very funny,' I said.

Then suddenly Leo's face became more serious. 'You know Simon would have been embarrassed by your spaghetti eating too, don't you?'

I looked at him, feeling confused. 'Well,' I said, 'I don't think he would.'

'Of course he would,' Leo said.

'He would not!' I argued.

'You just think he's so great you don't want to think

anything bad about him,' Leo told me.

'That's not true,' I said. 'I know Simon, that's all. He wouldn't be like that. He's a really nice man, and he likes me.'

Leo looked annoyed. 'Why are you girls always so blind when it comes to good looks?' he asked. 'Anyone can see that the man is only interested in himself! He's completely selfish.'

'Simon was very disappointed he wasn't coming on this date!' I said angrily.

'I expect he was,' Leo said. 'But that doesn't mean anything. The man has no heart. He's as thin as ... I don't know, a piece of paper.'

'Simon isn't ...' I began, but Leo interrupted me.

'Oh, I don't mean *physically* thin,' Leo said. 'The man's body is perfect, I'm sure. It's his brain that worries me – his brain and his heart. In my opinion, they're both rather empty.'

'Well,' I said, 'I disagree completely.'

'That's OK,' said Leo. 'You're allowed to disagree.' He paused, and then looked at me. 'I'm right though; you'll see.'

Things were difficult between us after this conversation. I was quite pleased when the secret door to the room opened again and the date was over.

Pete laughed when Leo and I came out of the Diary Room. 'Have you two had a food fight?' he asked.

I put a hand up to my tomato-red face. I'd been so busy being cross with Leo, I'd forgotten all about the messy spaghetti.

'In a way,' answered Leo, looking at me.

'Did Big Eye forget to provide knives and forks?' Simon asked, looking at my red face.

Straight away my face went even redder. I avoided looking at Leo. 'Leo and I just had a bit of fun,' I said.

'It doesn't look like much fun to me,' Nigel said. 'That spaghetti will make a lot of mess in the shower.'

Leo began to laugh. 'We'll see, shall we?' he said, and he walked off towards the bathroom.

'That's not very polite,' Pete said. 'He didn't ask you if you wanted to use the shower first, Annie.'

'Leo's *not* a lot of things,' Simon said. 'He's not polite, he's not active, he's not a good cook, he's not funny ...'

'Oh, Simon,' Pete said, 'I just can't agree with you there. Leo's definitely funny.'

Yes, I thought. He is funny. Very funny. And suddenly I felt ... well, a bit sad. It had been a really nice evening until Leo and I had argued. I wished we hadn't.

'Well,' Simon was saying. 'It's Leaving Night tomorrow – someone's going to go. We'll see what the public thinks, won't we? If they agree with me that Leo isn't funny, that he's just *annoying*, then he'll be leaving the House.'

We were always nervous on Leaving Night, although we all tried to hide it in different ways. Simon was normally out jogging right up until Big Eye told him to sit on the sofa. That's where we had to be to hear the result of the vote. The rest of us sat about and laughed – usually about something Leo had said. We pretended we didn't have a care in the world, when in fact we were all worried. None of us wanted to leave the House.

This Leaving Night was different. Leo had been quieter than usual all day, and things were still a bit difficult between him and me. Nigel was still looking bad-tempered with me, I thought, so he wasn't saying very much. Pete was the only person in a good mood, but even he had run out of things to say. So we were a very quiet – and probably very boring – group as we waited to be told who was to leave.

It was a warm night, and the doors to the garden were open. Every Leaving Night there was a large crowd of people outside. They came to see the person who was told to leave the House, and it was always noisy. That night it was *very* noisy indeed. We could hear people shouting, but we couldn't hear what they were shouting about.

It was very strange, sitting there on the sofas, waiting to see if you would be the one chosen to go. You thought about walking out there in front of all those shouting people. You thought about all the cameras pointing at you, and all the questions you'd be asked. Waiting for the result of the vote was like waiting for an exam result.

On Leaving Nights I also always thought about my family and friends and my life outside the House. I missed them, so every time I wasn't chosen to leave I felt a bit sad. Even though I was happy to be staying. I expect that sounds a bit crazy, but it's difficult to describe exactly what it was like.

That Leaving Night, I was trying not to think about anything. But it's hard to think about nothing, so I thought about the present I'd received that morning instead. Yes, another present – a smiling face made out of a round piece of soap! Very simple, but it had made me smile.

Nigel hadn't been smiling though. He'd come into the kitchen wearing only a towel. 'Who's hidden the soap?' he'd asked crossly.

So, I thought, it's not you leaving me presents.

Nigel still looked cross as we waited that evening

on the sofas for Violet Carlton to speak to us. We all knew she was outside the House in the crowd. We would know who was leaving any minute.

I looked up and saw that Simon was looking at me. 'I hope you don't go, Annie,' he said with a smile.

'It might be *you* going,' Leo told him.

'Don't start arguing again, you two,' Pete began to say, but at that moment Violet Carlton spoke to us.

'Big Eye House,' she said, 'this is Violet.' The sound of the crowd outside was very loud. Violet almost had to shout for us to hear her. 'The votes have been counted. The public has made a decision. The person who will be leaving the Big Eye House tonight is ...' Violet always paused before she told us the name. It made it more exciting for the people watching the TV programme. '... Nigel!'

We all looked at Nigel. He smiled, but his face was red.

'Nigel,' Violet said, 'you have five minutes to say goodbye to everybody and to pack your bag.'

Nigel got to his feet. We all looked at him. 'It's all right,' he said, before we could say anything. 'I'm happy to go. I've had enough of this place!' And he went off to the bedroom to pack his suitcase. Five minutes later, he was gone.

'So,' said Pete with a smile. 'Now there are only four of us.'

Nobody answered. We were too busy listening to the shouts of the crowd as the doors opened and Nigel walked out.

Chapter 6
Food and jumping

'Big Eye would like you to decide on a task for the three men who are left, Annie,' Big Eye told me. It was a man this time. 'Once again, it should be something to show how they feel about you.'

I'd been in the pool when Big Eye had called me into the Diary Room. So now I was sitting in my swimsuit, making the chair wet.

I didn't want the men to have to do another task about me. But I knew Big Eye wouldn't change his mind, so I didn't complain. Instead, I sat there and thought about what I could suggest.

That morning I'd received another present. It had been a plate of fruit, probably arranged in the shape of a face or something. But unfortunately it had fallen onto the floor when I woke up, so I wasn't sure. I still wanted to know who was leaving the presents for me. Maybe I could choose a task that would help me to find out who it was.

'OK,' I said to Big Eye. 'I've got an idea for a task.'

'Would you like to tell me your idea, Annie?' Big

Eye asked.

'I'd like them to make something for me,' I said. 'I don't mind what it is – they can make what they like. But it should be a thoughtful gift – something they think I'd really like.'

There was a pause. I waited, imagining the different Big Eyes discussing my idea.

'Big Eye accepts your idea for today's task, Annie,' Big Eye said at last. 'Please go and tell the men what they have to do. They have two hours before they have to present their gifts to you. While they are preparing their gifts, you should wait in the bedroom.'

Great – two boring hours on my own in the bedroom. Still, it would be worth it if I discovered who was leaving me the presents.

* * *

'What sort of thing do you want us to make?' Simon wanted to know after I'd told them about the task.

'That's your decision,' I told him. 'Big Eye wants it to be something that will show how you feel about me. I think you should try to think of something I need or something you know I would like.'

Simon and Pete looked thoughtful. Leo was smiling. 'Have you already got an idea?' I asked him.

His smile grew. 'Perhaps,' he said.

'This is Big Eye,' Big Eye said. 'Today's task will now begin. Annie, please go to the bedroom.'

'Good luck!' I said and I went off, wondering if my plan would work. I really wanted to find out who was leaving me the presents.

* * *

At one o'clock, Big Eye told me to go into the living area. When I got there, I found that only Pete was there. I could see the others outside, in the pool. Leo saw me and gave me a wave through the window.

'What's going on?' I asked Pete.

He smiled at me. 'Big Eye has asked me to present my gift first,' he said.

I smiled back at him, looking around the room. 'Right,' I said. 'Where is it then?'

'Over here,' Pete said. 'If you'd like to come this way?' Pete led me to the dining table, where I saw two – very large – plates of food waiting for us. 'I decided to make you lunch,' Pete told me. 'My mum has always said that the way to someone's heart is through their stomach!'

'Yes,' I said, not knowing *what* to say. To tell the truth, I wasn't feeling very hungry. It was a hot day, and Pete had cooked meat, potatoes and vegetables. I would have preferred a salad. 'My grandmother used to say that too,' I said.

'Well,' Pete said, still with that big smile, 'let's hope it's true!'

I sat down in front of one of the plates of food. Did Pete really want to find the way to my heart? Did he really want me to like him in that way – as a girlfriend? He hadn't given me any sign of it before. He'd always been very nice to me, but he was nice to everyone. He was like a friend, not a boyfriend. Maybe he was one of those men who can't show how they feel very easily.

'This looks ... lovely,' I said bravely, picking up my knife and fork. 'Have you always enjoyed cooking?'

'Oh yes,' Pete said, and he began to tell me all about how he had learnt to cook, what he liked cooking best, his cooking mistakes ... I listened, nodding every now and then as I chewed my food. Every time he stopped speaking, I asked him another question to get him to start talking again. I suppose I wanted to take his attention away from me, because I knew I definitely didn't want him to think of me as a girlfriend. I just didn't feel that way about him, and I didn't want him to be the person who was leaving me the presents.

After I had eaten as much as I could – which was

just under half of the food on the plate – I smiled at Pete.

'Thanks so much, Pete,' I said. 'That was delicious. But perhaps I'd better go and see what Simon and Leo have made for me now.'

'But the meal isn't over yet!' Pete said, jumping up. He went over to the freezer and came back with two very large bowls of ice cream.

By the time I finally went out into the garden, I was feeling a bit sick.

'Hello, Annie!' Simon said, getting out of the pool. 'Ready for my gift?'

'She looks as if she needs a rest first,' Leo laughed.

'Of course she doesn't need a rest!' Simon said, drying himself with a towel.

At any other time I'm sure I would have enjoyed watching Simon drying himself, but not then. 'Well, actually ...' I began, but Simon was already throwing the towel down and walking towards me.

'Come on,' he said, taking my arm. 'We've got work to do.'

He wasn't joking. Simon's gift to me was a physical training plan. 'You're not fat, of course,' he said, 'but everybody needs to keep their body in good condition.

Just do what I do.' And Simon began to jump and to run and to stretch. I did my best to follow what he was doing, but it was hot, and my stomach was full of food. Simon did everything very quickly as well. He was always moving on to a jump before I had finished a stretch, or to a stretch before I had finished a jump.

'I'm sorry, Simon,' I kept on saying.

'That's all right,' he said. 'You're doing fine.'

But I wasn't, and Leo clearly found it all very amusing. He was sitting on the edge of the pool smiling, and – when I actually fell over once – laughing. I was starting to get really angry with him. Simon was obviously getting angry with him as well, because suddenly he stopped jumping and reached out to push Leo into the pool.

But Leo found this even more amusing – he was still laughing when his head came out of the water.

'Everything's a joke to you, isn't it?' Simon said angrily.

But Leo couldn't speak. He was laughing too much.

I thought Simon might jump into the pool to hit him, but instead he looked at me. 'Well,' he said, 'that's my gift to you, Annie. If you do that every day your body will soon be in excellent condition.'

I was so tired I could hardly speak. 'Oh,' I said. 'Thank you. Thank you very much, Simon.'

'Don't mention it,' Simon said politely. 'Right, if you'll excuse me, Annie, I'll go inside for a shower now. If I stay out here any longer, I might do something to shut Leo up for ever.'

I watched him walk off, and then I sat down in a garden chair. Leo was still laughing.

'Shut up, Leo!' I said with my eyes closed.

I heard him come and sit in the chair next to me. 'I'm sorry,' he said, 'but you have no idea how funny that was!'

'Oh,' I said weakly, 'I think I do. And if your gift is anything to do with food or physical improvement, then you can forget it!'

'My gift is about improving your mind,' he told me.

'Improving my mind?' I repeated tiredly. 'What *can* you have made for me?'

'I've made you a questionnaire,' Leo said. 'A list of questions for you to think about and answer.'

I looked at him. 'Questions about what?' I asked.

Leo smiled. 'About you,' he said.

'Me?' I asked.

He nodded. 'Yes,' he said. 'They're designed to make

you think about what you want from life, and exactly how happy you are at the moment.'

'And this questionnaire is something you think I would want, is it?' I asked him.

'You said the gift should be something you would like or something we thought you needed,' he reminded me.

I was fed up. Pete had thought I needed food, Simon had thought I needed to work on my body, and now Leo thought I needed to work on my mind. Nobody seemed to be happy with me just as I was. And I still had no idea who was leaving me the presents.

'Go on then,' I said unhappily to Leo. 'Show me this questionnaire of yours. I'll try to answer your questions.'

Chapter 7 Questions, questions

In the end, Leo read the questions out to me.

'Right,' he said. 'Question number one. If you had one year left to live, what would you do?'

'That's a difficult one!' I said.

'They're all difficult,' Leo told me cheerfully.

'Oh, I don't know,' I said. 'Give up my job? Travel the world? Does anybody know what they'd do unless it actually happened?'

'Question number two,' Leo went on. 'What three things do you think you *must* do before you die?'

'Are all the questions about death?' I asked him.

'Not all of them, no,' he said. 'Come on, three things.'

'All right,' I said. 'Let's see.' Actually, it wasn't a difficult question to answer. I just felt a bit silly sharing my very private secrets with everybody. 'I'd travel the world, I'd have a child with the man of my dreams and I'd buy a house.'

'In that order?' Leo asked.

'Well,' I said, 'I suppose it would be best if the house came before the child.'

'And the man of your dreams came before the child?' Leo joked.

'Very funny,' I said. 'Come on, next question.'

Leo looked down at his piece of paper. 'OK,' he said, 'now we move on to your job. Question number three is what's the worst thing about your job and question number four is what's the best thing about it?'

'Well,' I said, 'I suppose the worst thing is that it's quite similar every day. The same old routines week after week. And the best thing ...' I paused, realising that my boss might be watching the programme. Or, if he wasn't, then somebody else who worked at the museum probably was.

'Come on,' Leo said. 'Tell the truth.'

'OK,' I said. 'I suppose the best thing about my job is getting my salary paid into my bank at the end of every month.' I looked at Leo. 'That's not very good, is it?'

'Well,' said Leo, 'it moves us on nicely to question number five – if your dream job would be to travel the world photographing and writing about beautiful things and places, then why aren't you doing it?'

'Because I can't afford it, I suppose,' I said. 'Or I'm just not brave enough or ambitious enough to take the first step. I don't know.'

Leo looked at me. I expected him to say something about my answer, but he didn't. 'OK, question number six,' he said instead. 'When are you going to take a photography course?'

I had intended to start one the year before, *and* the year before that. But I hadn't. 'In the autumn, I expect,' I said. 'Honestly, Leo, do you know how fed up this questionnaire of yours is making me? I feel like a complete failure.'

Leo didn't seem to care. 'It's all for your own good,' he told me. 'Right; this is the final question.' He paused, looking at me.

I was feeling annoyed with him by now. Why did he feel it was his job to make me think about all this stuff? OK, so I probably did need to think about it; no, I *definitely* needed to think about it. I was at a crossroads in my life and I needed to make some decisions. But I didn't need to do it in front of millions of television viewers.

'What sort of man do you think would be the

perfect boyfriend for you?'

I smiled. It was nice not to have to think about my job any more. 'Oh,' I said, 'that's easy. My perfect boyfriend would be a kind man. Someone who enjoys life, but who really cares about what he does. Someone who enjoys doing the same kind of things I do.'

'So,' Leo asked, 'he doesn't have to be good-looking then?'

'Well ...' I said, 'no, but I'd need to find him attractive.'

Leo laughed. I looked at him. 'I don't see why that's funny,' I said.

'It's not,' he said. 'You're just being honest.'

'You wanted me to be honest, didn't you?' I said. 'And anyway, I'm sure you haven't had any girlfriends you didn't find attractive.'

'Of course not,' Leo said.

'Well then!' I said.

'But they weren't all perfect either,' Leo said. 'Sometimes I find the way someone laughs attractive. Or the way they smile. The way they love life. There just has to be *something*, that's all.'

I looked at Leo crossly. 'First it was careers advice, and now it's relationship advice. And yet you're single, aren't you?'

'Yes,' said Leo.

'And you've been single for some time?'

'Yes,' said Leo.

'So you don't know everything then, do you?' I asked. 'If you did, you'd be attached by now.'

'I never said I did know everything,' Leo said.

I looked at him. 'You always have to have the last word, don't you?' I said. 'You *have* to win an argument.'

'Are we having an argument?' Leo asked.

My head was starting to hurt. 'Go away, Leo,' I said, and closed my eyes.

There was the sound of paper moving about. 'I was going anyway,' Leo said.

'Good,' I said, and when I opened my eyes next, I was alone. The questionnaire was on the chair next to me.

Immediately I felt guilty about being bad-tempered with Leo. It wasn't his fault that his questions had made me feel bad. I felt bad because I wasn't completely happy with my life at that moment, and his questions reminded me of that. I felt stuck, but I couldn't seem to do anything about it. That's why I'd wanted to come on this show – to do something – anything – different. And it certainly *was* different.

'Hi.' I looked up at the kind voice and smiled. Pete was standing next to me. 'Mind if I join you? If you'd rather be alone, just say.'

I did want to be alone, but I couldn't say so. Pete was just trying to be nice, and I didn't want to hurt him as well as Leo. 'No,' I said, 'that's OK.'

'Are you feeling tired after your day?' he asked.

I smiled again. 'Yes!' I said. 'I certainly am. My head hurts. And my legs.'

'What about your stomach?' Pete asked.

'Well,' I said, 'I don't want to eat anything else until tomorrow! I'm very full.'

Pete laughed. 'Sorry,' he said. 'I did cook a lot of food, didn't I?'

'Enough for about six,' I said.

'I come from a large family,' Pete told me. 'I'm used to cooking big meals.'

'It was a lovely meal, Pete,' I told him. 'And it was a great idea for a present.'

I smiled, and we sat in silence for a while. Somewhere a bird was singing. It was quite peaceful, and I felt myself begin to relax. I closed my eyes to do a bit of sunbathing.

'I wonder what the next task will be?' Pete said.

'I don't want to think about it!' I said, still with my eyes closed.

'Tomorrow evening there'll only be three people here,' Pete said.

'Oh yes,' I said. 'I'd forgotten about that. There's another Leaving Night tomorrow.'

'Yes,' Pete said. 'But none of us has much longer in here. We'll all be returning to our normal lives soon.'

I didn't want to go back to my normal life. Leo's questions had made me recognise how unhappy I was with everything. The question was: what was I going to do about it?

'Well,' I said, making an effort to be cheerful, 'I hope it's not you who goes.'

Pete looked at me. 'Really?' he said. 'You'd prefer it to be one of the others?'

I opened my eyes, thinking about it. I definitely didn't want it to be Simon who left. And as for Leo ... I wasn't sure about Leo. He could make me feel tired, but did I really want him to leave? Actually, for some strange reason, I didn't.

I smiled at Pete. 'I don't want any of you to go,' I said.

'One of us will have to,' he said.

'That's true,' I agreed. I looked at him, thinking again what a nice man he was. 'You really like what you do, don't you?' I asked.

'Being an engineer?' Pete said. 'Yes, I love it.'

'What do you like best about it?' I asked, thinking of Leo's questionnaire.

Pete didn't need to think about it. 'I like seeing what I've helped to make, after it's finished,' he told me. 'A bridge or a building – you stand and look at it and you think, I helped to make that. It's a good feeling.'

'It must be,' I said.

We were quiet for a while. I imagined Pete standing there looking at one of his buildings with a big smile on his face. I certainly never smiled like that after a group of schoolchildren left the museum these days. I had when I'd first started the job, I supposed.

'You don't ever get bored with building bridges then?' I asked Pete.

'No,' he said. 'Every bridge is different.'

'That's great,' I said. 'You're very lucky.'

Pete paused for a moment, then he asked, 'Would you like to come and see one of my bridges after this is all finished?'

'I'd love to ...' I started to say, but then I turned

and looked into his face. There was something about the way he was looking at me which made me wish I hadn't answered so quickly.

Pete reached out to touch my hair. Suddenly, his face seemed very close to mine. 'I'd like to think we could spend some time together after this is over, Annie,' he said. 'Lots of time ...'

I was completely surprised by Pete's change of mood, and while I tried to think of something to say, his face was getting closer and closer. *He was going to kiss me!*

Suddenly I jumped to my feet. 'Sorry, Pete!' I said quickly. 'I've got to ... to ... use the bathroom.' And I ran indoors.

Chapter 8
Kisses

'Big Eye House, this is Violet,' Violet Carlton told us the following evening. 'The person who will be leaving the Big Eye house tonight is ...'

Over on the other sofa, Pete avoided my eyes. He'd been doing that most of the day. Neither of us had spoken about what had happened in the garden. Leo and Simon had been around, and there hadn't been a chance for Pete and me to be alone. But that morning, as I made my way to the bathroom, we had met face-to-face.

'Pete,' I had said, 'about yesterday ...'

'Forget it,' he had told me quickly. 'I was silly to think you'd be interested in being my girlfriend.' And with that he'd walked away, leaving me wondering if I was to blame in any way. I didn't think I'd done anything to make Pete believe I found him attractive. I'd told him I hoped he wouldn't be leaving the House, but I'd just been making conversation. Oh dear, perhaps it was my fault.

'... Pete,' Violet Carlton finished.

'Of course,' Pete said, and stood up. Leo and Simon went over to him to shake his hand. I stood up too, but I didn't go over. I wasn't sure if Pete would want me to. I was sorry Pete was leaving. He was a very nice man, and, although I didn't want him to be my boyfriend, I did like him.

'Bad luck,' Leo said.

'That's OK,' Pete said. 'It was always going to be me next. You two are strong, attractive characters – you were never going to be voted out until the end.'

'What about me?' I said, and finally Pete looked over at me.

'Oh no, Annie,' he said. 'It couldn't be you. The public want to keep you here. They want to see a romance.' He came over to me and took hold of my arms, looking down into my face. 'And anyway, you're pretty, funny, caring ...' He paused to smile at me. 'The list goes on. Anyone who *does* have a romance with you will be a very lucky guy – in here or in the outside world.' And while I was busy taking all of this in, Pete kissed me.

Five minutes later, his bag was packed, and he was waiting for the doors to open.

'Pete,' said Violet Carlton, 'you must now leave the

Big Eye House.'

The doors began to open. Pete picked up his bag and then looked at Simon and Leo seriously. 'You'd better make sure you're good to Annie,' he told them. 'I'll be watching you.'

Then he walked through the doors. They closed after him. Simon, Leo and I stood there, waiting for the screams and shouts to begin when the outside doors to the building opened. There were stairs outside our exit – when you left the House you had to walk up the stairs and then other doors opened to let you outside.

Suddenly the noise from the people waiting outside started up – a big wall of sound. It didn't matter how often I heard it, it still always came as a surprise.

'Goodbye, Pete,' I said softly.

Beside me, Leo yawned and gave a big stretch. 'Leaving Night makes me very tired,' he said. 'I think I'll have a rest.' And off he went, leaving me alone with Simon.

Simon sat down on one of the sofas. I went to join him. 'That man needs to see a doctor,' he said.

I looked at him. 'Who? Pete?' I asked.

'No, Leo,' Simon said. 'He's always having to have a sleep. Though now I come to think of it, Pete should probably go and see a doctor too. He's clearly feeling very sick. Very *lovesick*.'

'Stop it,' I said. 'I feel as if I'm to blame somehow. And yet I don't think I did anything to make him believe I felt that way about him. But I still feel guilty.'

'Don't,' Simon advised me. 'You can't help being pretty, funny and caring, can you? It's not your fault if people fall for you.' He looked at me and took my hand in his. 'He was right about all those things, by the way.'

I felt suddenly hot and looked down at my hand in his. 'Oh,' I said. 'Do you really think so?'

'Yes,' Simon said, 'I do. Although I think he left one important thing off his list. You're also very sexy. Especially with bolognese sauce on your face.'

I looked up at him. 'You're laughing at me,' I said.

Simon smiled. 'Only a little,' he said. 'And only because I like you. I'm very, very happy that out of all the women you're the last one in the House.'

I didn't know what to say. I felt happy and embarrassed all at the same time. 'That's very nice of you, Simon,' I said.

'I'm not saying it to be nice,' Simon told me. 'I'm saying it because it's how I feel.'

I didn't know what to say. Simon hadn't paid me

this amount of attention before. It was making me nervous to have him sitting so close to me, looking right into my eyes. He was a very attractive man, and I was feeling the effects of having him so near me. It was a bit like being hit by a train.

'Er ... thank you,' I said nervously, looking at his mouth and wondering if he were going to kiss me in front of millions of viewers. Pete had kissed me, it was true, but that had been different. That had been a goodbye kiss, but this would be ... well, to be honest, I wasn't sure. A 'hello' kiss? The start of a relationship?

The silence stretched on. The moment probably only lasted a few seconds in reality. But sitting there, with Simon looking down at me like that, it felt as if it lasted for *years*. I had to say something, *do* something, or my heart would stop.

I opened my mouth to speak. I had no idea what I was going to say. 'We'd ... we'd better start making dinner, I ... I suppose,' I said.

Simon looked at me. It obviously wasn't what he'd expected to hear. 'Funny little Annie,' he laughed softly. 'Thinking about food at a time like this.'

A door opened somewhere behind us. 'Did someone mention food?' asked Leo in a bright voice. 'I am *so* hungry. What are you going to cook, Annie?'

* * *

'And how are you feeling this evening, Annie?'

I'd been in the Diary Room for about twenty minutes. I'd come to have a bit of time to myself. I know that probably sounds crazy, but it was Simon and Leo I wanted to get away from, not Big Eye or the people watching on TV. What would have happened if Leo hadn't come into the living area talking about dinner and being hungry? Would Simon have kissed me? Did I want him to kiss me? I'd liked the look of Simon from the first moment I saw him. Of course I wanted him to kiss me. Didn't I?

'I'm feeling ... confused,' I told Big Eye.

'Why is that, Annie?' Big Eye asked. Big Eye was a woman that night. 'I'm not sure what I think about anything,' I told her. 'Everything's mixed up in my mind.' I felt a bit sad, and I could tell it showed in my voice. 'I've realised I'm not happy with my life outside here, but I'm not sure what to do about it. I don't feel ready to leave here yet. Does that sound stupid?'

'Do you think it sounds stupid, Annie?' asked Big Eye. I'd forgotten that Big Eye never, ever gave opinions.

'A bit, yes,' I said. 'But I can't help it. That's the way I feel. And it's not helping having Simon and Leo arguing all the time.'

'Why do you think they're arguing, Annie?' Big Eye asked.

'I suppose they're very different,' I said. 'And they're both people who think they're always right.'

This was followed by one of Big Eye's pauses. I wondered if Simon and Leo were still arguing. I wondered if either of them had done anything about dinner. Probably not. That was one way Simon and Leo were similar – they both seemed to think that cooking was women's work.

'Have you discovered who has been leaving you presents yet, Annie?' Big Eye asked.

'No,' I said. 'I haven't. But if there isn't one tomorrow morning, then I'll know it was Pete. I don't think it was Pete though. Actually, I'm thinking of staying awake all night tonight. I thought I might be able to surprise the person who's leaving the presents.'

'And if you do surprise them, what will you ask them?' Big Eye asked.

'Why they're doing it, I suppose,' I said. 'I mean, is it just a game? Or are they leaving presents because they care for me?'

'Have you thought of asking who's leaving you the presents?' Big Eye asked.

I shook my head. 'I feel shy about asking,' I said. 'I don't know why. I'd prefer to catch them doing it.'

There was another pause. I imagined myself lying in the darkness waiting for either Simon or Leo to bring me a present. I would have to drink some very strong coffee before I went to bed so that I stayed awake.

'Who do you want the person leaving you these presents to be, Annie?' asked Big Eye.

It was the question I hadn't wanted her to ask me. It was the question that was confusing me the most at the moment. 'I don't know,' I said.

There was another silence before Big Eye spoke. I chose not to break it. 'Big Eye wishes you luck, Annie,' she said finally.

I did my best to smile. 'Thank you,' I said. 'Will I have to think of another task before the final Leaving Night?'

'Big Eye has chosen a task for tomorrow evening,' Big Eye told me. 'You will all receive your instructions for it tomorrow afternoon.'

'I can't wait,' I said, not totally truthfully. I half got up from the chair. 'Right,' I said. 'I'd better go and see to tonight's dinner. Thank you for listening to me, Big Eye.'

'You are welcome to talk to Big Eye at any time, Annie,' Big Eye reminded me.

'Thank you,' I said to her, and then I left.

To my surprise, Simon was in the kitchen making a meal when I left the Diary Room. Leo was in his usual place on the sofa. He looked deep in thought, and I wondered if he was thinking about his next story.

'Dinner will be ready soon, Annie,' Simon told me with a smile.

'Great,' I said. 'It smells lovely. Do you want me to lay the table?'

'Yes, please,' Simon said.

I went over to the drawer where the knives and forks were kept and got some out. Simon looked over. 'We'll only need two of those,' he said.

I didn't understand what he meant. 'What?' I asked.

'We'll only need two knives and two forks,' Simon told me. 'I've just cooked enough food for you and me.'

'Oh,' I said, surprised.

Across the room, Leo was looking a lot more than

surprised. 'Haven't you made enough food for me?' he asked.

'No,' said Simon unpleasantly, 'I haven't. I promised Annie we would do something special together when you won that stupid poetry competition. This is our "something special". You can make your own food.'

'Why didn't you tell me earlier?' Leo said crossly.

'You didn't ask,' Simon said. 'This isn't a restaurant, you know!'

Another argument! Maybe it wouldn't be such a bad thing when all of this was over after all.

'I'm sure there'll be enough for all of us,' I said. 'I don't need a big meal.'

But Simon wasn't going to change his mind. As I watched, he carried a saucepan over to the table and began to put the food onto two plates. 'Come on, Annie,' he said. 'Bring the knives and forks. We don't want it to get cold.'

So, for the second time in two days, I sat down to eat a meal that had been specially prepared for me by a man. I now knew that Pete had wanted to show me his feelings with his food. Was it the same with Simon?

And what was going to happen *after* the meal?

But nothing happened after the meal. It couldn't

because Leo didn't leave Simon and me alone. All the time we were eating, Leo was singing loudly as he made himself a sandwich. A sandwich he brought over to the table to eat.

When Simon made coffee for us and suggested we drink it outside in the garden, Leo soon followed with his own cup of coffee and sat down near us.

'Do you mind?' Simon said to him angrily.

'Not at all!' Leo said cheerfully.

'I meant, do you mind moving away? Annie and I would like some space.'

'Actually,' I said. 'I was just going in to make some more coffee.'

Simon looked surprised. 'Have you finished that one already?' he asked.

I'd remembered my plan to stay awake that night. 'Yes,' I said. 'Do either of you want another cup?'

'No, thanks,' said Simon.

'OK then,' said Leo. 'Very kind of you to offer, Annie.'

And as I went back inside, I could hear the pair of them start to argue again. They were like children.

When I took the coffee out, Leo pulled a face when he drank his. 'This is strong!' he said. 'Do you want us both to be up all night or something?'

I didn't reply, and soon after that Leo was called to the Diary Room.

'Alone at last!' said Simon, moving his seat closer to mine and reaching out to take my coffee cup away.

This time Simon didn't give me a chance to talk about food or even to think. He began to kiss me straight away. It was a very nice kiss, a very nice kiss indeed. But although I enjoyed it, I'm afraid there was a part of me that felt terribly embarrassed about the millions of viewers watching me and Simon kissing. My mum watching me and Simon kissing! But I hoped very much that Janine and Gloria were watching. Especially Janine. She would be *so* jealous!

At last Simon broke away to look down at me. 'Sweet little Annie,' he said softly. I think he was going to kiss me again, but at that moment Leo returned.

'Oh, sorry,' he said. 'Did I interrupt something?'

Before Simon could answer, I got to my feet. For some reason, I badly needed to escape. 'Actually,' I said, 'I was just on my way to bed. See you in the morning.'

I did go to bed, although I wasn't at all tired. I suppose that was partly because of the strong coffee, but also I couldn't stop thinking about Simon kissing me. I'd liked Simon for ages. He'd always been friendly towards me, but he hadn't given any sign that he wanted to be more than a friend before. His feelings towards me seemed to have changed. It was very confusing.

After about an hour, the others came to bed. I still wanted to find out who was leaving me the presents. Tomorrow was the last day, so if I didn't find out by the morning, I might never find out. I kept myself awake by thinking about the museum. I played a game, imagining each room in the museum and all the things in it. If I made a mistake and forgot something, I had to start again. There are a lot of things in the museum, so this kept me busy. But as time went past, it got more and more difficult to stay awake.

I only realised I'd fallen asleep when something woke me up. Someone was getting out of bed. I kept perfectly still, waiting for whoever it was to come over to my bed to leave a present. But he didn't come over; instead, he left the bedroom. When he returned two minutes later and got back into bed, I realised he must just have needed the bathroom.

The next thing I knew, all the lights were on and I was alone in the bedroom. It was morning, and by the looks of things, I had overslept. Feeling annoyed with myself, I looked down on my bed to see if there was anything there. There was something. I picked it up and looked at it. It was a key, cut out of paper. A key. What a strange present. What did it mean? And who had left it? Simon or Leo? Was I ever going to find out?

Chapter 9
Truth dancing

Saturday – the last day in the House – was a long day. I felt strange being around Simon after that kiss. I wasn't sure what to say to him. I didn't know what the kiss had meant, and I felt confused. But I was never alone with him anyway. Leo was always there. I don't think any of us could believe it was our last day in the House.

Finally, in the afternoon, Big Eye called Simon into the Diary Room to give him the instructions for the final task.

'Right,' he said to Leo and me when he came out. 'The final task is a dance competition between me and Leo.'

'You mean you and I have to dance together?' asked Leo.

Simon looked annoyed. 'Of course not! We both dance with Annie. She learns the tango with me, and the jive with you.'

I was immediately worried. 'Wait a minute,' I said. 'I'm not a very good dancer. I can't learn both the tango and the jive!'

Simon smiled at me. 'You'll be fine with me,' he said. 'I *am* a good dancer.' He looked back down at his piece of paper. 'Leo and I each have an hour's practice with you, and then the actual competition begins at seven o'clock.'

'But how will we learn the dances?' I asked. 'Do you know how to tango?'

'No,' Simon said. 'But Big Eye has provided us with instructions for both dances. I'm sure it won't be difficult to learn.'

'Well, I can't do the jive either,' said Leo. 'And guess what? I'm sure it will be *very* difficult to learn. I'm a useless dancer.'

'Oh dear,' said Simon with an unpleasant smile. 'I *am* sorry to hear that. Come on, Annie, we might as well start now.' Without waiting for me to say anything in reply, Simon stood up and walked towards the kitchen area. 'The floor in here will be excellent for dancing.'

I got up slowly. I didn't want to do it. I knew I was about to look stupid in front of millions of viewers. Again. I'd been telling the truth when I said I wasn't a good dancer, a fact Simon was about to find out for himself.

'Don't let him order you about too much,' Leo advised me.

I didn't like to smile at him because Simon was looking cross. 'Annie is going to have fun,' he said.

'That's order number one, Annie,' Leo told me.

'I suggest you study your instructions, Leo,' Simon said, and then he turned his back on him, bending his head over his own instructions.

While I waited, I tried to remember what I knew about the tango. I knew it was from Argentina, and a bit like a piece of theatre. I'd seen it danced on television before, but I had never, ever dreamt of trying it myself.

'Right,' said Simon to me after a few minutes. 'In the tango the man and woman have to hold their bodies very straight, and they move with quick, sudden movements.' Simon held his back very straight to show me what he meant. 'It's a dance about sex.' Behind him, Leo laughed, but Simon pretended not to hear. 'Sometimes it can even be about murder,' he continued. 'It's always a dance about fire and heat. But the most important thing of all is that neither the man nor the woman must *ever* smile. They must remain serious at all times.'

That was the hardest thing for me to do, as we were learning the dance. Oh, the dance steps were hard enough – I wasn't good at them at all. But I was really hopeless at staying serious.

'It isn't funny, Annie,' Simon told me over and over again. 'I don't know why you're laughing.'

'I'm sorry,' I said. 'It's probably because I'm nervous. I always laugh when I'm nervous.'

'Well, try a little harder, please,' he said.

So I tried, but it was no good. When Simon looked at me as if he wasn't sure if he was going to kiss me or kill me, I couldn't help laughing again.

Simon looked cross. 'Are you sure you're trying, Annie?' he asked.

'Yes,' I told him. 'I really am.'

'Well, try even harder,' he said. 'I told you: this dance is about sex and murder. It's serious.'

I did try, very hard. But I was so busy thinking about not laughing, I got the steps all wrong.

'No!' Simon said, clearly very fed up with me by then. 'Not like that, like this! I thought we'd learned that bit!'

'I'm sorry,' I apologised again. And again. By the end of an hour I badly needed to take a rest. But Simon wanted to carry on practising.

'I need to sit down, Simon. My feet hurt,' I tried to tell him, but he wouldn't listen.

'In a minute,' he kept saying. 'Let's just go over the last bit again.'

I don't know how long it went on for, but then suddenly Leo reappeared and came over. 'Your time's up, I think,' he told Simon, leading me away towards the sofas.

'There you are, Annie,' he said. 'Put your feet up.' After I had taken my shoes off my poor, hurting feet, I did just that.

I didn't say anything for a while. I was too busy thinking. The dance practice with Simon had been really unpleasant. Simon hadn't seemed to care about me being tired. He'd just gone on and on, telling me what to do and complaining when I got it wrong. I'd never thought about it before, but Simon was a bit like my boss, Mr Penforth. He expected me to work very long hours, and for no extra pay too.

'I still have to learn the jive with you,' I told Leo at last.

'It's OK,' Leo said. 'We'll just make it up.'

I suppose he was just being nice because he knew I was tired, but suddenly I felt annoyed with him.

'Don't you want to win?' I asked him.

And suddenly I realised I often felt annoyed with Leo. It was because I wanted him to ... well, to *want* things more, I suppose. He didn't really seem to care about anything very much. But he must care about his writing, because he was successful at it. He couldn't be successful if he didn't care.

'I'm never going to win a dance competition against Mr Perfect over there,' Leo said.

'You might,' I told him, standing up. 'Don't be so pessimistic. Come on; you should at least try.'

'Oh, OK then,' he said.

So we began to practise, and it couldn't have been more different to dancing with Simon. With Simon it had all been very serious. I'd felt afraid of doing anything wrong. But with Leo it was completely different. We got it wrong all the time, but we laughed about it.

'Sorry!' said Leo every time he stood on my feet.

'Not so fast!' I cried, as he danced us in a circle so quickly the room started to go round and round.

As dancers, we were hopeless, but it was great fun. I hadn't laughed so much since the spaghetti dinner.

But eventually practice time was over, and we had to get ready for the real thing. The competition started as arranged by Big Eye, at seven o'clock. Once again, we were given clothes to wear. My dress was black with a big skirt that moved around my legs as I moved. I loved it. Simon had tight black trousers and a tight black shirt and looked extremely handsome. Leo ... well, Leo had a tight *pink* shirt and tight *pink* trousers and looked ... stupid. Really stupid. Simon did all that exercise and looked after his body. But Leo was tall and thin with a bit of a stomach. The pink did not look good on him at all, and he knew it.

I tried not to laugh, but I just couldn't help it. Simon laughed too. 'You look like some kind of animal that lives under the ground,' he told Leo unkindly. 'A worm, that's what you look like. A worm!'

I watched Leo's face. For just a very short time he looked hurt. But then he laughed. 'Oh well,' he said, 'I always did like worms.'

'Me too,' I said. It wasn't the truth, but I just wanted to say something nice to Leo. I'd suddenly realised how very much I liked him. Oh, he annoyed me, and I wished he would be a bit more active, but I really liked him. And suddenly I knew I wanted *him* to win the dance competition, not Simon. Unfortunately, I knew that wasn't likely.

'The dance competition will now begin,' Big Eye

told us. 'Annie will dance the tango with Simon first.'

Simon stood up and waited for me to join him. As he held me in his arms and we waited for the music to start, I looked up into his face. I don't know what I expected to see, but it wasn't what I saw. Simon's face was as empty as a piece of wood.

This time I didn't laugh once as I danced the tango with Simon. He was very pleased with me after we'd finished.

'That was great, Annie!' he told me at the end. 'I'll definitely win now!'

'Let's just enjoy ourselves,' Leo told me when it came to the jive. So that was what we did. We made mistakes and we laughed; we even put in some steps of our own that hadn't been in the instructions. It was great fun, but it wasn't the dance Leo had been told to do. I knew he would almost certainly lose the dance competition.

All three of us went to sit on the sofas to wait for Big Eye to speak to us.

'This is Big Eye,' Big Eye said. 'The result of the dance competition is to be decided by a public vote. We will tell you who the winner is at nine o'clock this evening.' There was a pause before Big Eye spoke again, and then what he had to say made us all look at each other with surprise. 'The loser of the competition will leave the Big Eye House tonight.'

Chapter 10 Winners and losers

None of us could believe it.

'That's not fair,' Simon said. 'Still, I shall still win. It will be obvious to the public that I'm a better dancer than you, Leo.'

Leo just looked at him.

'And then, Annie, it will just be you and me,' Simon said with a smile in my direction.

Suddenly I knew I didn't like that idea much at all. Oh, it was true that Simon was good-looking, and he could certainly kiss well. But I couldn't help thinking how horrible he'd been to Leo about his dancing clothes. And how he'd ordered me about when we'd been learning the tango. If we were left alone together in the House, I wasn't sure I would be able to think of anything to say to him.

The time until nine o'clock passed very slowly. And then finally Violet Carlton spoke to us.

'Big Eye House, this is Violet,' she said. 'The votes

have been counted. The person who has lost the dance competition and who is to be the next person to leave the Big Eye House is ...'

Simon was sitting up very straight on the sofa. Leo was half lying, with his hands behind his head. I was moving my foot up and down impatiently. The waiting moment seemed to go on for ages and ages.

'... Simon!' Violet finally finished.

I was looking at Simon's face as Violet spoke so I saw it turn red when he heard his own name.

'Simon,' Violet continued, 'you have five minutes to pack your bag and say your goodbyes.'

I stood up and moved towards him. 'Oh, Simon,' I said. 'I'm so sorry.'

'Yeah,' said Leo. 'You were definitely the best dancer. I'm sorry.'

Simon looked at him. 'You aren't sorry at all,' he said coldly. 'We've hated each other from the start. I don't see any need to pretend to like me just because I'm going.'

Leo nodded. 'Fair point,' he said.

Simon got to his feet. 'If you want to know the truth, I can't wait to get out of here,' he said. 'And do you know what? I don't care if I never see either of you again.' And off he went, heading towards the bedroom.

I stared after him. I couldn't believe what I'd just heard. If Simon felt like that, then what had that kiss been about? I began to walk after him.

'Leave him, Annie,' Leo advised me. 'He's obviously a bad loser.'

'No,' I said, walking on. 'I want an explanation.'

In the bedroom Simon was throwing his clothes into his suitcase. He didn't look up when I went into the room.

'You were pretending, weren't you?' I said. 'Pretending to like me.'

'Not really,' Simon said, sounding bored. 'I didn't *dislike* you. To be honest, I didn't think much about you at all until all the other girls had gone. After that, well, £80,000 seemed a lot better than £70,000, I suppose.'

'So you tried to use me!' I said angrily. 'Thanks very much!'

Simon closed his suitcase and picked it up from the bed. Finally he looked at me. 'A word of advice, Annie,' he said. 'Don't ask questions if you don't want to hear the answer.' And then he walked out.

Two minutes later, he was gone from the House –

and my life – for good. Which left Leo and me on our own.

'Are you OK?' Leo was sitting on one sofa, and I was on the other. We could still hear the crowd outside. They'd gone really wild when Simon had left the House.

Leo and I were sitting quite a long way away from each other, but we were close enough for me to realise he was worried about me.

'Yes,' I said. 'I'm OK.' And I was OK. Maybe Simon had tried to use me, but it didn't matter. I wasn't really hurt, because I now knew I hadn't had any deep feelings for him.

Once I'd begun to compare Simon to Mr Penforth, my boss, I couldn't stop. Simon always thought he was right about everything, just as Mr Penforth did. Simon was nice to me when it suited him. That was just like Mr Penforth too, when he wanted me to work at the weekend, for example.

I had *really* liked Simon, but now I knew that I hadn't seen the real Simon at all. I'd just seen his good looks; that was all. But I was beginning to understand that good looks weren't that important. It was what sort of person you were that mattered.

'What you said about Simon at our spaghetti dinner,' I said to Leo now. 'You were right.'

Leo smiled. 'Ah,' he said. 'The spaghetti dinner. That was a good night.'

I remembered the spaghetti in Leo's hair and smiled. 'Yes,' I agreed. 'It was.' I looked at him. 'How did you see what Simon was really like?'

'There are lots of people similar to Simon in the writing world,' he told me. 'People who like you while you're at the top and successful. But if your next book is a failure, they don't want to know you any more.'

'False friends,' I said, and he nodded.

'Yes,' he agreed. 'But if I'm honest, I was jealous of Simon too. He's attractive and confident, and women always prefer a man like that.' He laughed at himself. 'I'm as useless with women as I am at dancing. That's why I'm a writer. Writing's easy. You can make the detective catch a murderer or the guy get the girl. Reality is much harder.'

I looked at him, realising something. 'You make a joke out of everything,' I told him. 'Why do you do that?'

'To avoid getting hurt, I suppose,' Leo answered.

'Does it work?' I asked.

'I suppose so, yes,' Leo said. 'Because it stops people getting close to me. But just lately I've been learning that it's not always a good thing to avoid being close to people.'

It was the most serious conversation I'd ever had with Leo. I wanted to ask what he meant, but Big Eye interrupted our conversation. 'This is Big Eye. The public vote to decide the winner of the Big Eye competition is now taking place. The result will be given in fifteen minutes.'

Leo and I looked at each other. Fifteen minutes. *Fifteen minutes*. If I won the competition or not, I would soon have to return to my normal life. And I might never see Leo again. Suddenly I felt really sad.

'Well,' said Leo, 'it's almost the end.'

'Yes,' I said. 'I ... I'm sorry it's ending.'

I wanted one more night of talking to Leo – one last opportunity to find out about the real man behind the jokes.

I wanted to wake up the next morning to see if somebody had left me a present. Because if I woke up and found a present, then it would definitely be from Leo. And I knew suddenly that I really, really wanted it to be Leo who had been leaving me the presents.

I liked Leo very much. We'd always got on well, but I'd confused those feelings for simple friendship. Leo and I *were* friends, but for me it was more than that.

'I'm sorry it's ending too,' Leo told me quietly, and suddenly I couldn't think of anything to say to him. Now I had finally realised how I felt about him, I felt shy.

There are only a few minutes left, I told myself. Say something now before it's too late.

But it was already too late.

'Big Eye House, this is Violet,' Violet Carlton said.

This was it. The result.

Leo and I looked at each other. I wanted to go and sit next to him – to hold his hand or something – but I felt too shy to do it.

'The votes have been counted, and I can now tell you that the winner of the Big Eye competition is ...' As usual, Violet paused. This time the silence seemed to last ages. Then, finally, Violet spoke again: '... Leo!'

I jumped to my feet. 'Oh, Leo!' I said. 'Congratulations!' I was so happy for him. I ran over to him, wanting to kiss him or take him into my arms, but Leo just sat there. He didn't look as if he could believe it.

'Annie,' Violet continued, 'you have lost the Big

Eye competition and must now leave the Big Eye House. You have five minutes to pack your bag and say your goodbyes. I'm coming to get you.'

'I ... I'd better go and pack,' I said to Leo. When Leo didn't answer, I went to the bedroom as if I were in a dream. Leo had won, not me, but I didn't care. I hadn't won the £70,000, but I didn't care about that either. I'd never expected to win. But now I would have to walk up those steps from the House and face that crowd. Violet would interview me on television. But, worst of all, I still hadn't told Leo how I felt about him. Perhaps I should do it now, before I left.

But when I went back into the living area, Leo was sitting exactly where I'd left him. He didn't look like a man who had won a big prize.

'I can't believe it,' he told me. 'It must be a mistake.'

'It's no mistake,' I said. 'You heard what Violet said. You've won.'

'But why?' he said. 'Why would they vote for me?'

I knew this might be the only chance I'd ever get to say how I felt. 'Because you're funny,' I said. 'And kind.'

'No, I'm not,' said Leo.

I smiled at him. 'Well,' I said, 'you can be. You

were very kind to me on our spaghetti date. If you want to, you can make people very happy.' You make me happy, I was going to add, but once again it was too late.

'Big Eye House,' said Violet, 'this is Violet. Annie, you must now leave the Big Eye House.'

The doors began to open. Leo got to his feet. 'I don't understand why you didn't win,' he told me.

'No,' I told him. 'The public chose well.'

'Annie, please leave the Big Eye House,' said Violet.

I picked up my bag. 'Goodbye, Leo,' I said.

'Yes,' he said. 'See you on the outside.'

I nodded, and then I walked through the doors. They closed quickly behind me. I walked nervously up the steps. When I reached the top, the outside doors opened, and as I walked through them, a wall of sound met me.

'Annie! Annie!' the crowd shouted. 'Annie! We love you!'

Nothing like it had ever happened to me before in my whole life, and I knew that nothing like it would ever happen to me again. I felt ... like a film star.

Then Violet was there, and she was reaching out to give me a kiss.

'Annie!' she said. 'Smile for the cameras!' And I

did smile, and the night sky was lit up as hundreds of photographers took pictures of me.

We walked, Violet and I, through the crowd of screaming people, and I didn't know if I wanted to laugh or cry. If they were like this for me, the person who had lost the competition, what would they be like for Leo, the person who had won the competition?

Leo. What was he feeling right at this moment?

I was soon to find out. Violet and I sat on chairs in front of the TV cameras. And there, on a very big television, was Leo, still dressed in pink, sitting in the House on his own. His face was in his hands. He looked ... alone.

'Poor Leo,' Violet said. 'Look at him! You've been gone for five minutes and he's already missing you like crazy!'

'He can't believe he's won,' I said, but Violet shook her head.

'No, that's not what's wrong with him, Annie,' Violet said. 'He's missing you. I know it, the whole country knows it, and after you've seen this, you'll know it too.'

Violet pointed to the television. The picture changed from Leo, sitting alone in the living area of the House. There were lots of pictures of Leo run together to tell the story of his time in the House. But every single piece of film was about me too.

There were Leo and me playing with our spaghetti and laughing. Leo asking me his questions from his questionnaire. Leo and me laughing as we danced the jive really badly. Lots of things I knew about already. But there were other things too, things that I didn't know about. Leo looking cross when Simon was telling me what to do. Leo watching jealously from the living area as Simon kissed me. Leo in the Diary Room.

'I can't stop thinking about her,' he told Big Eye. 'She's funny, intelligent ... beautiful too, only she has no idea about that. She's always saying how hopeless she is. We're actually quite similar in lots of ways, but I don't think she's realised it yet.'

'Will you tell Annie how you feel, Leo?' Big Eye asked.

'What's the point? She won't look at me while Mr Perfect is still in the House.' Leo smiled. 'I've never been in love before. It really hurts, doesn't it? Still it will be a very useful experience for my writing.'

And lastly there was the film shot at night with the special cameras. Leo putting a paper boat on my bed. The carrot flower. The soap. The fruit face. The paper key. And every time he stood and looked down at me with ... well, with love.

The film ended. Violet looked at me, and I realised my face was wet with tears.

'That is so sweet,' Violet said. 'The man has been crazy about you since Day One. How did it make you feel, watching that, Annie?'

'Sad,' I said. 'Happy. I ... I don't know. I just wish he'd said something instead of wasting all this time. I had no idea he felt that way about me.'

'What would you say to him now, if you could speak to him?' Violet asked.

I didn't need to think about it. 'I'd tell him I love him,' I said.

It was the answer the crowd had wanted to hear. They let out a big scream of pleasure as I spoke. Violet was smiling all over her face. 'Well,' she said, 'I think it's time you said just that. I shall speak to the Big Eye House.'

'Big Eye House,' she said, 'this is Violet.'

On the television, Leo looked up.

'Leo,' Violet said, 'Annie wants to say something to you.' And she looked at me and nodded.

I looked at Leo on the television. He was looking

right back at me, and it felt as if he could see me. At the last moment, I changed my mind about what I was going to say. 'Leo,' I said, 'why did you make me that key? What was it supposed to mean?'

Leo smiled for the first time since he'd been told he'd won the competition. 'Well,' he said, 'that depends on what you want it to mean. It could just be a key to an exciting new career, or ... it could be something totally different.'

It didn't seem as if millions of people were listening to our conversation. It felt as if it was just Leo and me. 'Like what?' I asked.

Leo looked nervous. 'Like ... the key to my heart,' he said softly. 'To my heart and my love.'

He'd said it without making a joke and without laughing. And I knew then that he'd decided to take a chance. To give somebody – me – the chance to get close to him.

'It depends which you prefer,' he said. 'The choice is yours.'

If he'd been able to see me, he would have known that I was crying with happiness. It was such a powerful feeling, I felt as if I might explode with it. 'Then,' I said through my tears, 'I choose heart, please. Heart and love. Definitely.' And then I was laughing and crying at the same time, sitting there watching the biggest of smiles on Leo's face, and everybody in the studio was crying too. Even Violet.

'Big Eye House,' she said in a shaky voice, 'this is Violet. Leo, you have won the Big Eye competition. Get ready. We're coming to get you!'

And she took my hand and we ran back out through the screaming crowds.

'Annie and Leo!' they shouted so loudly it made my ears hurt. 'Annie and Leo!'

And then the Big Eye House doors were opening, and there he was, the competition winner, holding out his arms to me. And as I ran into them, I knew I was just as much a winner as he was.

After reading

读后活动

1. Write a paragraph saying which character you liked best and which least, and explain why.

2. Write a physical and character description of either Leo, Simon or Annie.

3. Think of another title for *In the House* and explain why it would be good.

4. If you were making a film of this story, which famous actors would you choose to play the main parts? Explain who and why.

5. Write an email to the author, Margaret Johnson, saying what you did and didn't like about the story.

6. What do you think about this kind of reality TV programme? Write a paragraph expressing your views.

7. You are Leo. Explain how you feel at having won the contest and Annie.

8. Write Annie's diary saying what she and Leo do in the first week after leaving the House.

Learning guide | 学习指导

Chapter 1

New words 生词

- admit /əd'mɪt/ *v.* 承认
- anonymous /ə'nɒnɪməs/ *a.* 匿名的；名字不公开的
- gown /gaʊn/ *n.* 长袍，长外衣
- intelligent /ɪn'telɪdʒənt/ *a.* 聪明的
- jog /dʒɒg/ *v.* 慢跑
- instruction /ɪn'strʌkʃn/ *n.* 命令；指示
- mystery /'mɪstəri/ *n.* 神秘；秘密；迷
- odd /ɒd/ *a.* 古怪的
- presenter /prɪ'zentə/ *n.*（广播、电视）节目主持人
- romance /rəʊ'mæns/ *n.* 恋爱；爱情
- yawn /jɔːn/ *n.* 哈欠 *v.* 打哈欠
- vote /vəʊt/ *v.* & *n.* 投票，选举

Phrases & expressions 短语和表达

- dress up 打扮，装饰；盛装打扮
- fall over 跌倒，摔倒
- or rather 更精确地说，倒不如说
- prefer ... to ... 比起……，更加喜欢 / 宁愿……
- take the trouble to do sth. 不辞劳苦地做某事
- wear out 磨损，用坏；穿破

Reading exercises 阅读练习

1. Who is narrating this story?
2. Why are five of the beds in the bedroom empty?
3. Read the information on Page 5 again. How many more days are there for the people to stay in the house?
4. Which statement is true?
   a) Simon has left a carrot on Annie's bed.
   b) Leo has carved a carrot.
   c) There is a flower carved out of a carrot on Annie's bed.
   d) There is an orange flower on Annie's bed.
5. Who does Annie go to talk to and in which room?
6. What is the day's task?

Chapter 2

New words 生词

- co-operate / kəʊˈɒpəreɪt / *v.* 合作
- crossly /ˈkrɔːsli/ *ad.* 生气地，发怒地
- deafening /ˈdefnɪŋ/ *a.* 震耳欲聋的
- detective /dɪˈtektɪv/ *a.* 侦探的
- edge /edʒ/ *n.* 边缘
- explode /ɪkˈspləʊd/ *v.*（使）爆炸；（使）爆发
- hoover /ˈhuːvə(r)/ *n.* 吸尘器
- inspire /ɪnˈspaɪə(r)/ *v.* 激发；鼓舞
- kettle /ˈketl/ *n.* 壶
- mug /mʌg/ *n.* 杯子
- photography /fəˈtɒgrəfi/ *n.* 摄影；摄影术

- plug /plʌg/ *n.* 插头
- poetry /ˈpəʊɪtri/ *n.* 诗；诗歌
- sigh /saɪ/ *v.* & *n.* 叹息；叹气
- sociable /ˈsəʊʃəbl/ *a.* 社交的；好交际的；友善的
- stuff /stʌf/ *n.* 东西

Phrases & expressions 短语和表达

- get away with ... 侥幸逃脱……
- hold onto ... 紧紧抓住……不放
- no wonder 难怪，不足为奇
- there is no point in (doing) sth.（做某事）毫无意义
- to be honest 说实话，老实说

Reading exercises 阅读练习

1. How does Annie feel about being in the house and in front of the cameras all the time?
2. The four men are very happy about writing the poem. True or false?
3. Match the beginnings and endings:

   ______ 1) Nigel thinks

   ______ 2) Leo is

   ______ 3) Simon says

   ______ 4) Annie does

   ______ 5) Janine did

   a) Annie has to stay inside while they write.

   b) it isn’t fair to be asked to write a poem.

   c) some cleaning while they are writing the poems.

   d) the cleaning before she left the house.

e) a writer of detective novels.

4. Who has a lot of accidents?
5. What do they have to wear for the poetry competition?
6. When Annie reads the first poem

a) who is embarrassed?

b) who laughs so much?

c) who smiles?

Chapter 3

New words 生词

- disappointed /dɪsəˈpɒɪntɪd/ *a.* 失望的，沮丧的
- doubtful /ˈdaʊtfl/ *a.* 可疑的；疑心的
- frighten /ˈfraɪtn/ *v.* 使惊吓；吓唬
- murder /ˈmɜːdə/ *v.* & *n.* 谋杀，凶杀
- oven /ˈʌvn/ *n.* 烤炉，烤箱

Phrases & expressions 短语和表达

- as for ... 至于……，关于……
- (be) fed up with ...（对……）感到厌烦
- go off sb. 对某人失去兴趣
- if only 要是
- in turn 轮流，依次
- let go of ... 放开……

Reading exercise 阅读练习

Put the events in the correct order:

_______ a) Big Eye tells them that the winner will have a date with Annie.

_______ b) Simon goes to complain to Big Eye about the competition.

_______ c) Leo is the winner.

_______ d) Annie reads the other three poems.

_______ e) Simon is affectionate with Annie.

_______ f) Annie chooses the winning poem.

_______ g) Annie makes fun of Nigel.

Chapter 4

New words 生词

- attempt /ə'tempt/ *v.* & *n.* 企图，试图，尝试
- behaviour /bɪ'heɪvjə(r)/ *n.* 行为；习性
- bolognese /ˌbɒlə'neɪz/ *n.* 意式肉酱
- character /'kærəktə(r)/ *n.* 角色；性格，品质；特性
- equal /'iːkwəl/ *v.* 等于；比得上 *a.* 平等的；相等的
- impatiently /ɪm'peɪʃntli/ *ad.* 没耐心地；不耐烦地
- spaghetti /spə'geti/ *n.* 意大利面

Phrases & expressions 短语和表达

- end up 结果是；结束
- fall off 跌落，掉落
- might/may as well 还是……好

- spaghetti bolognese 意大利肉酱面，意大利番茄牛肉面
- take a bite 咬一口

Cultural note 文化点滴

• mummy: 木乃伊，即“人工干尸”。此词源自波斯语 mumiai，意为“蜡”。古埃及人笃信人死后，其灵魂不会消亡，仍然会依附在尸体或雕像上，所以，法老、贵族等死后，均被制成木乃伊，而普通老百姓是没有机会成为木乃伊的。

Reading exercises 阅读练习

1. Leo and Annie have their date
   a) in the Diary Room.
   b) in a restaurant.
   c) in a secret room.
   d) in the House dining room.
2. How is Annie's character described in two words? '__________ and __________'.
3. Which of these things happen to Annie while they have dinner or happened in the past?
   a) She spilt soup on her dress.
   b) She crashed her car into a tree.
   c) She locked two boys in a room at the museum.
   d) Her bikini top came off.
   e) She lost her handbag.
   f) She got fruit juice on her arm and nose.
   g) She dropped a bowl of peas.
   h) She broke a mirror.

4. Why is spaghetti a bad thing for Annie to eat?
5. What does Leo decide they should do with the spaghetti?

Chapter 5

New words 生词

- bad-tempered /ˈbædˌtempəd/ *a.* 脾气不好的；易怒的
- exhausted /ɪɡˈzɔːstɪd/ *a.* 疲惫的；耗尽的
- selfish /ˈselfɪʃ/ *a.* 自私的；利己主义的
- sexy /ˈseksi/ *a.* 性感的；迷人的

Phrases & expressions 短语和表达

- get to one's feet 站起来
- run out of ... 用尽……，用光……

Reading exercises 阅读练习

1. Who says these things?
   a) 'Why are you girls always so blind when it comes to good looks?'
   b) 'That spaghetti will make a lot of mess in the shower.'
   c) 'Leo's not a lot of things. He's not polite, he's not active, he's not a good cook, he's not funny ...'
   d) 'I hope you don't go, Annie.'
   e) 'The votes have been counted. The public has made a decision.'
   f) 'I'm happy to go. I've had enough of this place!'
2. Why do Leo and Annie argue at dinner?
3. How do the contestants feel on this Leaving Night?

4. Why is it noisy outside the House?

Chapter 6

New words 生词

- amusing /əˈmjuːzɪŋ/ *a.* 有趣的，好玩儿的
- chew /tʃuː/ *v.* 咀嚼；细想，深思
- freezer /ˈfriːzə/ *n.* 冰箱
- questionnaire /ˌkwestʃəˈneə/ *n.* 问卷
- stretch /stretʃ/ *v.* & *n.* 伸展，张开
- thoughtful /ˈθɔːtfl/ *a.* 深思的；体贴的

Phrases & expressions 短语和表达

- every now and then 不时地，常常
- in good condition 情况良好

Reading exercises 阅读练习

1. Who do you think made the plate of fruit and the other presents Annie finds on her bed each morning? Give reasons for your opinion.
2. What task does Annie invent for the men to do?
3. Who ...
   a) makes food for Annie?
   b) does something for her body?
   c) does something for her mind?
4. Who pushed whom into the pool and why?
5. What sort of questionnaire do you think Leo has produced for

Annie?

6. How does Annie feel about Pete?
   a) She wants him to become her boyfriend.
   b) She doesn't like him at all.
   c) She thinks of him as just a nice friend.

Chapter 7

New words 生词

- ambitious /æmˈbɪʃəs/ *a.* 野心勃勃的；有雄心的
- attach /əˈtætʃ/ *v.* 使依附；贴上；系上；使依恋
- cheerfully /ˈtʃɪəfəli/ *ad.* 高兴地
- relationship /rɪˈleɪʃnʃɪp/ *n.* 关系；恋爱关系
- routine /ruːˈtiːn/ *a.* 日常的 *n.* 日常工作
- sunbathe /ˈsʌnbeɪð/ *v.* 沐日光浴

Phrases & expressions 短语和表达

- have the last word 强辩到底；有决定权；最后说一句
- jump to one's feet 跳起来，一跃而起

Reading exercises 阅读练习

1. In general, how would you describe the kind of questions Leo asks Annie?
2. How does Annie react to the questions? She finds them
   a) interesting and helpful.
   b) helpful but annoying.
   c) annoying and stupid.

3. How does Annie say she feels about herself because of the answers she gives?
4. What makes Annie angry with Leo?
5. Which of these words and phrases does Annie actually use to describe her life?
   a) unhappy with everything
   b) very dissatisfied
   c) stuck
   d) bored with everything
6. In what ways is Pete similar to how Annie describes her 'perfect boyfriend'?
7. What surprises Annie at the end of the chapter?
8. Who do you think will be voted out of the House next?

Chapter 8

New words 生词

- jealous /ˈdʒeləs/ *a.* 嫉妒的，妒忌的；猜疑的
- oversleep /əʊvəˈsliːp/ *v.* 睡过头
- saucepan /ˈsɔːspən/ *n.* 深平底锅

Phrases & expressions 短语和表达

- fall for sb. 爱上某人
- in reality 实际上，事实上；在现实中
- mix up 混淆
- see to sth. 关注某物，留意某物
- take hold of ... 握住……

Reading exercises 阅读练习

1. Put these events in the correct order.

_______ a) Annie talks to Big Eye in the Diary Room.

_______ b) The three contestants go into the garden to drink coffee.

_______ c) Pete leaves the House.

_______ d) Simon makes dinner for just Annie and himself.

_______ e) Simon kisses Annie.

_______ f) Simon tells Annie he finds her attractive.

_______ g) Leo is called to the Diary Room.

_______ h) Annie goes to bed.

_______ i) Leo and Simon argue in the garden.

2. Why does Pete think he has to leave the House, not Leo or Simon?
3. What plan does Annie make to find out who is leaving the presents? What happens?
4. What do you think the paper key means?

Chapter 9

New words 生词

- arrange /əˈreɪndʒ/ *v.* 安排
- pessimistic /ˌpesɪˈmɪstɪk/ *a.* 悲观的；消极的
- reappear /ˌriːəˈpɪə(r)/ *v.* 再出现
- worm /wɜːm/ *n.* 虫，蠕虫；小人物

Phrases & expressions 短语和表达

- dream of ... 梦想……，向往……

- make ... up 弥补……
- order about ... 驱使……，不断差遣……

Cultural notes 文化点滴

- jive: 牛仔舞，又称捷舞，拉丁舞项目之一。牛仔舞原是美国西部牛仔跳的一种踢踏舞，在第二次世界大战期间，由美国水兵传播开来。这是一种节奏快、耗体力的舞。
- tango: 探戈。一种双人舞蹈，源于非洲，但流行于阿根廷。目前，探戈是国际标准舞大赛的正式项目之一。

Reading exercises 阅读练习

1. Who said these things?
   a) I'm not a very good dancer.
   b) I *am* a good dancer.
   c) I'm a useless dancer.
2. What are the characteristics of the tango, according to Simon?
3. How would you describe Simon's behaviour when they are learning to tango?
4. How does (a) Leo describe Simon as a dancer and (b) Annie describe Simon's face when they are starting to dance?
5. How is dancing with Leo different from dancing with Simon?
6. Why are they all surprised by what Big Eye says?
7. Who do you think the people will vote out of the House and why?

Chapter 10

New words 生词

- dislike /dɪsˈlaɪk/ *v.* 不喜欢，厌恶
- explanation /ˌekspləˈneɪʃn/ *n.* 说明，解释
- shaky /ˈʃeɪki/ *a.* （身体、声音）颤抖的

Phrases & expressions 短语和表达

- for good 永远，永久地
- let out 释放；发出
- light up 点亮
- take a chance 冒险；碰运气

Reading exercises 阅读练习

1. Which of these statements is true? Simon is angry about leaving the House because
   a) he loves Annie and wants to stay with her.
   b) he knows he danced better than Leo.
   c) he is a bad loser.
   d) another reason (what?)
2. Why did Simon kiss Annie?
3. What does Annie realise about her view of other people when she finds out about Simon's behaviour?
4. What does Leo say about why he makes a joke about everything?

5. Put the adjectives in the box into the correct sentences.

shy kind happy sorry nervous

a) Annie was very ________ when she walked out of the House.

b) Both Annie and Leo were ________ the contest was ending.

c) Annie didn't hold Leo's hand because she felt ________ .

d) Annie said Leo was very ________ to her at the spaghetti date.

e) Leo made Annie feel ________ because of his behaviour on the date.

6. How does Annie feel when she goes through the crowd outside the House?

7. What does she find out about Leo from Violet?

8. How does Leo explain the meaning of the key to Annie? Did you guess correctly in Chapter 8?

9. Why does Annie say she was a winner, as well as Leo?

Translation 参考译文

屋下爱情

第 1 章　胡萝卜花

第5页

并不是每天醒来你都会发现床上有胡萝卜的，但这事就发生在我待在大眼屋里的第 36 天。

噢，准确地说，它不是一根胡萝卜，而是一朵花，一朵用刀在一根胡萝卜上精心雕刻出来的花。我知道这听起来有点儿奇怪，但说实话，它真的很漂亮。我很高兴某人不辞劳苦地为我做这个东西。不过我不知道这个“某人”会是谁，然而我清楚自己希望他是谁——西蒙。西蒙有一双好看的手，还有一副好身材和一张帅气的脸。可是他那双手能做出这样的花来吗？我希望能。

我环顾了一下卧室，看到利奥还躺在床上。大眼屋里有一间卧室供我们所有人住，里面有十张床。然而，没有人会再使用其中的五张床了，因为有五个人已经离开了大眼屋。我看着熟睡的利奥。大眼每天早上八点会打开卧室的灯，但这却没有吵醒利奥。什么也叫不醒利奥，除非他自己想醒。所以，我觉得胡萝卜花肯定不是他做的。不管怎样，他是不会做这种事情的。利奥更喜欢空谈而不是行动。

第6页

突然，一个声音在屋子里响起来："我是大眼。请安妮到日记室来一下好吗？"

日记室是我们跟大眼进行私密谈话的地方。哦，交谈之所以是私密的，是因为在大眼屋里的其他人听不到你说什么。但实际上谈话是很公开的，因为从电视上收看《大眼》节目的每个人都能看到你并听到你所说的话。不过，你通常会忘记这一点。

我穿上晨衣后，小心翼翼地把胡萝卜花放进口袋里。出于某种原因，我想保守这个秘密，尽管我知道这样做很傻，因为成千上万，甚至可能是数百万的电视观众已经看到我发现它了。

"早上好，各位。"在外面的主生活区，皮特和奈杰尔正在做早餐。他们冲着我微笑。

"早上好，安妮。"

当我走向日记室时，我看着他们俩。奈杰尔是一个很聪明的人，但他的双手不是很灵巧。我无法想象他能够给我刻出一朵胡萝卜花来。皮特是一名工程师。也许会是他？

第7页

我朝窗外望去，寻找西蒙的身影。他在那儿，像往常一样在慢跑。每天早晨，他都会在早餐之前跑上一个小时。他已经把小花园里的草踩坏了一些。到周六比赛结束时，花园里大概就没草了。会是西蒙在他锻炼之余给我做的礼物吗？如果是的话那就太好了——实在是太好了。

我暗自笑着，按下了日记室门外墙上的按钮。我一边等着门开，一边继续观察着西蒙。假如看这个节目的女性和我一样的话，那西蒙和他那健美的身材绝对有机会赢得这场比赛。待在大眼屋里时间最长的人将赢得比赛，而且获胜者的奖金是七万英镑。现在离比赛结束只有四天了。

在“离别之夜”，成千上万的人会打电话给电视台进行投票——说出他们想让谁离开大眼屋。一开始，“离别之夜”每周六举行一次。已经有五个人离开了大眼屋。但现在比赛差不多要结束了，就另加了两次“离别之夜”。到周六，也就是比赛的最后一天，将只剩下三个人。

第8页

“离别之夜”总是千篇一律：大眼屋里的所有人都要坐在沙发上，等待电视节目主持人维奥莱特·卡尔顿来宣布我们谁将离开。到目前为止，西蒙一直是安全的——没有多少票是投他的。实际上也没有多少票投给我。几乎没有人打电话来说我们俩应该离开。我不知道为什么自己这么受欢迎。我长得不丑，但肯定也不漂亮。

当我听到日记室的门开始打开时，我还在盯着西蒙看。我开始走进房间，没有注意到门开得不够大，我无法进去。我的胳膊撞到了门上。

“哎哟！”我一边说一边捂着受伤的胳膊。皮特和奈杰尔看了过来。

“还好吧，安妮？”皮特问道。

“还好，”我说道，“只是又受了点儿伤。”所有的男士们已经习惯了我的各种意外。我总是会弄掉东西或者被什么东西绊倒。

当我坐在日记室的椅子上时，我仍然捂着我的胳膊。更精确地说，我是陷进了椅子里，因为它又大又柔软，你得半躺在上面。不放松的话，你根本无法坐在这把椅子上。我觉得大眼知道，如果我们放松的话，就会更坦率地说出我们的想法。

第9页

“早上好，安妮。”大眼说道。

我正打着哈欠。“早上好，大眼。”我微笑着对面前的摄像头说。大眼根据时间的不同，有四五种不同的声音。有时候大眼是个男的，而有时候大眼是个女的。今天早上的大眼是那个嗓音温柔的男士，他的声音像牛奶巧克力一样。我喜欢他。

“安妮，你今天早上感觉怎么样？”大眼问道。

“不错，”我仍然面带微笑说道，“事实上，非常好。”

“安妮，有什么特别的原因让你今天早上感觉这么好吗？”

我能用手摸到口袋里的那朵胡萝卜花。我知道大眼想要我谈谈它，但是我仍然想要保守这个秘密。“哦，我想，此时此刻这里的一切都很平静。”我说道。

“那你为什么这么认为呢，安妮？”大眼问道。

我想了想，说：“我想是因为贾宁和格洛丽亚走了。她们俩制造了很多麻烦。”

第10页

贾宁和格洛丽亚都很吵闹，是那种抢眼的人。除了获胜者获得奖金之外，在大眼屋里谈恋爱的任何人也将获得一万英镑。贾宁和格洛丽亚两个人都非常努力地想跟西蒙谈恋爱。

“还有什么其他原因让你今天早上感觉这么好吗，安妮？”大眼问道。

我盯着摄像头，看起来大眼不打算放弃。最后，我说道：“有。你知道有的。有人又给我送了礼物。昨天是那只漂亮的纸船，而今天是……这个。”我从口袋里掏出那朵胡萝卜花，用手拿到摄像头前。“很漂亮，对吧？”

大眼没有发表意见。大眼从不发表意见。“你知道是谁给了你这个礼物吗，安妮？”

我摇摇头说：“不，我不知道。这完全是个谜。我昨天试着找出是谁给我折的纸船，但没有人承认。所以，我不知道给我礼物的那个神秘人是谁。”这时，我意识到了什么，睁大眼睛看着摄像头说：“但你知道，对吗？你一定知道，你知道大眼屋里发生的一切。”

第11页

大眼屋里除了浴室和洗手间之外到处都有摄像头。那些摄像头甚至能在夜里看见我们——有一些特殊摄像头能在黑暗中工作。

“是谁啊？”我问大眼，“是谁一直在送我礼物？”

“大眼不能为你提供这个信息，安妮。”大眼说道。

“你的意思是你不想提供吧。”我说道。

大眼没说话。我把胡萝卜花放回口袋，猛然意识到（早上在喝一杯浓咖啡之前我的反应有点儿慢）如果大眼知道是谁给了我礼物，那么每个人就都知道了，也就是全英国正在收看《大眼》节目的所有人都知道。想到数百万人比我自己更了解发生在我身上的事情，我就觉得很奇怪。

“作为大眼屋里剩下的唯一一位女士，你感觉怎么样，安妮？”大眼问道。

我想了想说：“哦，我想我不再确定男士们对我的真实看法了。我的意思是，他们对我很好，但我怎么知道他们是不是真的喜欢我呢？也许他们对我好仅仅是因为他们想谈一场恋爱并赢得一万英镑。”

第12页

“那你觉得跟大眼屋里的某个人谈恋爱怎么样？”大眼接着问道。

我立刻想到了西蒙并暗暗笑了笑。“我不确定，”我对大眼说，“剩下的男士们都很不一样，对吧？他们每个人身上都有我喜欢的东西。”

谈话暂停了一下。大眼经常留下一些沉默的时间。他想让你感到不自在，这样你就会说点儿什么来打破沉默。我自己倒不介意沉默。我想这源于我在一家博物馆工作。博物馆是个非常安静的地方，尤其是在夏天。人们不喜欢在阳光明媚的时候去看老照片和旧家具。

“现在大眼要给你一些指令，安妮。”大眼说道。

“哦？”我说道，等待着。

“你要去告诉利奥、西蒙、皮特和奈杰尔，大眼希望他们为你写一首诗。这首诗应该表达出他们对你的感觉。”

“一首诗？”我说道，突然感到一阵恼火，因为我只能看着摄像头。我想能够盯着这位牛奶巧克力先生的脸。“你是说像这样的：

第13页

玫瑰是红的，
紫罗兰是蓝的，
糖果是甜的，
而你也是甜的？”

“每个人都可以决定自己想要写什么类型的诗。”大眼说道。

“他们会恨死这个任务的！”我说道，不期待出去告诉他们所有人。

大眼继续往下说，明显不担心男士们会怎么想。“他们必须在今天上午10:30之前完成他们的诗，”他说道，“11:00时你要把诗读出来并决定哪一首写得最好。诗必须是匿名的——任何人都不可以在诗上面署名，你也不应该知道是谁写的。这就是今天的任务。”

我们每天都被安排做一些事情——一项任务。这一部分原因是为了让我们忙个不停，但主要是为了吸引在家看电视的那些观众。有些人就是喜欢看我们打扫大眼屋或在花园里的泳池边上聊天。我不知道这是为什么，但是大多数人想要看我们做愚蠢的事情。在大眼屋里的这段时间，我和西蒙一起扮过一匹马，参加过一场歌唱比赛（我拿了最后一名），还在花园里打过一场女生对男生的水仗（男生赢了）。我们不得不按照大眼所说的去做——这都是大眼比赛的规则。

第14页

“大眼想要你现在就去告诉其他人今天的任务，安妮。”大眼对我说。我双手撑着从椅子上站了起来。

“那好吧，”我说，“再见。”

“再见，安妮。”大眼说道。

我离开了日记室，去把这个坏消息告诉大家。

第 2 章　像湛蓝的海水

第15页

很难形容住在大眼屋里面是什么感受。虽然你并没有完全忘记你在外面的生活——你的朋友、你的家人、你的工作——但是它们几乎就像是你听过的故事。大眼屋才是现实的生活——这里有房间、人，以及告诉我们该做什么的大眼。

大部分时间你甚至忘记了有摄像头这回事。我知道这听起来可能有点儿难以置信，但确实如此。那么多的摄像头，到处都是，记录着我们的一举一动、一言一语。但你对此已经习以为常，不再去想了。我们就像在碗里游来游去的鱼，只是我们看不到这只碗的外面，我们不知道外面的世界发生了什么。大眼屋以及在它里面发生的事情，就是我们的世界。这就是为什么像写诗这样愚蠢的比赛变得如此重要的原因。

当我宣布这个任务的时候，大家没有一个乐意的，而奈杰尔则特别恼怒。“这不公平！”在我描述完大眼让他们做什么时，他抱怨着说，“我甚至连购物清单都不爱写！我甚至不知道写一首诗怎么开头。况且他已经是一位作家了。”奈杰尔指着利奥——那个五分钟之前当大眼命令所有人到沙发上集合时才从床上爬起来的人。他正紧紧端着皮特给他冲的那杯咖啡，好像那是救命良药一样。

第16页

“我写的是侦探小说，不是诗歌。”他打着哈欠说道，“而且不管怎样，我必须是真正对什么东西感兴趣才会想要去写它。”

“你是说你需要灵感？”皮特问道。

利奥点点头，喝了口他的咖啡。“没错，我需要灵感。”

“那你觉得一具死尸比安妮更能让你获得灵感？”西蒙一边说一边朝我看来，“这可不太好，对吧，安妮？”

利奥笑着对我说：“不好意思，安妮，恐怕这是真的。血、恐惧与神秘——这些才是激发我灵感的东西。”

我感到很生气，但我尽量不表现出来。在大眼屋里的所有男士当中，利奥是那个最不努力讨好我的人。不过他对每个人都这样——利奥就是利奥，我们可以接受他，也可以不接受他。可是我们却莫名其妙地喜欢他。他非常善于交际，尽管有时他很懒，但他也很搞笑、有趣。我觉得利奥从来没有在与人交往上花太多心思。

第17页

“好吧，”我说道，“我希望你们大家配合一下。你们都要做这项任务，所以抱怨也没用。你们都清楚如果不去做这个任务会怎么样。”

“会没有好吃的。”奈杰尔说道。

大眼只给我们提供最基本的食物，比如面包、米饭和土豆，而我们必须通过成功完成这些任务来赢得更多的食物。

“今天是星期二哦。”奈杰尔继续说道。

“外卖之夜！”皮特说道。

在每个星期二，如果我们完成了任务，大眼就会给我们提供啤酒和一餐来自印度或中国餐馆的外卖。我们都喜欢外卖之夜，就连平时只吃健康食品的西蒙也不例外。

“那我们最好开始忙起来了！”利奥说完，端着自己的咖啡杯走回了卧室。

“别忘了——诗上面不能写名字。它们必须是匿名的。”我在他身后喊道。

其他人走到花园里。当我想要跟着他们时，西蒙叫我留在室内。“如果你在的话我就不能好好地思考了，”他说，“我会觉得自己太傻了。”

第18页

“我也是，”皮特表示同意，“对不起，安妮。”

“没关系，”我说，“我去打扫一下卫生。这里太乱了。”

的确是这样。贾宁是那个爱打扫卫生的人。当她没有费尽心思让西蒙跟她独处时，她就忙着用吸尘器吸尘或擦洗厨房的地板。当时是有点儿令人讨厌——你刚把咖啡杯放下，贾宁就会把它拿走洗干净。但是现在她不在我们身边，这个地方变得脏兮兮的，所以我很想念她。嗯，说实话，我是想念她干的活儿，而不是她这个人。她对我一点儿也不友好。

当我拿出吸尘器开始打扫的时候，我还在想着男士们听到写诗这个任务时的反应。他们都不想写。虽然我知道写诗不容易，但我确实觉得他们至少应该假装一下我是个写诗的好题材。可是事实上，他们全都抱怨这件事。利奥竟然说他宁愿写死尸。这些对一个女生的自信心来说都不是好事。

第19页

我在干活儿时太过于忙着为自己感到难过，以至于没有注意到正在发生的事情。吸尘器把地毯的边缘“吃”了进去，开始发出非常奇怪的声音。

“噢，天哪！”我焦急地说道，试着把吸尘器从地毯那里拉开，可是它却纹丝不动。地毯边缘卡到了吸尘器里面。噪声震耳欲聋——吸尘器听起来好像要爆炸了。我弯下腰去，想把地毯拽出来，但没成功。然后突然，吸尘器停止了轰鸣。

我四处望了望。利奥拔掉了吸尘器在墙上的插头，站在那里嘲笑我。“我知道我说过我的灵感来源于谋杀，安妮，”他说，“但那块地毯怎么惹你了？”

我看着他，由于感觉难堪就生气地问道：“你不是应该在写诗吗？”

利奥走到水壶边把它打开烧水。“写完了。”他说道。

我站起来，把吸尘器留在原地。一个早上的清洁工作已经让我受够了。“这有点儿太快了。”我说。

利奥只是笑了笑。“你要来一杯咖啡吗？”他问。

突然之间，一杯咖啡成了这世上我最想要的东西。我一直在想什么呢，竟然没有先喝杯咖啡就开始打扫卫生？怪不得全都出了差错。“哦，好的，请给我来一杯！”我说。

第20页

但是利奥已经离开了水壶，走到沙发那里坐了下来。“我的要放两块糖，”他说，“不要放太多的奶。”

“利奥！”我说，“我以为你要给我冲杯咖啡呢！”

他大笑起来。“我知道。”他说。

这就是利奥。我不知道他是怎么做到的。如果其他男生跟我开这样的玩笑，我一定会觉得非常生气。但是不知为什么，我发现自己跟利奥一起笑了，然后去冲咖啡了。要是有人能够干了坏事而不受惩罚，那一定是利奥。

“给你，”我端着咖啡回来说道，“你很幸运，我没把咖啡泼在你身上。”

利奥微笑着接过咖啡。“我的确幸运，不是吗？”他说，“毕竟在你身上发生了那么多意外事故。你是怎么做好你的工作的？”

“你是什么意思？”我问。

“哦，”他说，“博物馆里全是贵重的东西，对吧？而你总是出状况。你不会总是打碎东西吧？”

第21页

我曾经打碎一个相当古老的盘子，但我不打算告诉利奥和所有正在收看节目的人。我的老板还记得这事呢，而我也没忘。“我不经常碰博物馆里的东西，”我告诉利奥，“我的工作是向参观博物馆的成群的小学生介绍博物馆。”

利奥笑了。“你的意思是，你会说‘博物馆，这是来自福克斯伍德小学的玛丽、埃伦和彼得’？”他开玩笑地说。

“不是，”我耐心地说，“我的意思是我为孩子们组织一些活动——根据博物馆里的东西进行素描或绘画，或者在他们参观时提出一些问题让他们回答。”

如果让我说实话，这不是我一直想要的工作。虽然工作通常还说得过去——如果你没遇到一群调皮捣蛋的男孩子到处乱跑或躲在某个地方的话，但这并不是我大学毕业后所希望做的工作。

“假如你能做世界上的任何事情，你会做什么？”利奥问。而我立刻就回答了他，想都不用想。

“我会出国旅行拍照，写写美丽的事物和地方。”我说。

第22页

“你擅长摄影吗？”利奥问。

“不擅长，”我说，“目前还不擅长。”

利奥笑了。

“但是我可以学。”我告诉他。

“我是大眼，”大眼打断了我们，“所有的诗都必须在10:30之前写完。麻烦利奥到日记室来一下好吗？”

利奥抬头看着天花板，声音好像是从那里传来的。“我必须去吗？”他问，但大眼没有回答。“那我就当作是‘必须’去了。”利奥说道，叹了口气站起来。

他很快就回来了，怀里抱着很多衣服。“大眼让我领了这一堆东西。”他说。

“这是什么？”我惊讶地问。

“是你读我们写的诗时我们所有人要穿的衣服。大眼显然是要我们看起来精神点。”

我走过去看了看，是四套黑色西装和一件用闪亮的绿色布料做成的漂亮长裙。我摸了摸。“真漂亮！”我说。

“就你觉得漂亮！”利奥不高兴地说，“我只在婚礼上穿西装！”

到11:00时，男士们全都穿上了西装，而我穿的是那件绿色长裙。我还把头发盘了起来，感觉不错。

第23页

“你看起来很漂亮，安妮，”皮特说，“这个颜色真的很适合你。”

我冲他笑笑，想着他真是个好人。我从来没听他说过任何人的坏话，而且他总是乐于助人。“谢谢你，皮特，”我说，“你看起来也很帅，你们都很帅。”这是真的——他们都很帅。西装使他们全都看起来很英俊并且……嗯，我觉得更加成熟了。

“我是大眼，”大眼说道，“诗歌比赛将在两分钟后开始。请将所有的诗放进桌上的箱子里。需要提醒你们的是，诗必须是匿名的——你们的名字不应该出现在你们的诗上面。”

“或许你应该把脸转过去，安妮，”奈杰尔建议道，“这样你就看不到我们把诗放在箱子里了。”奈杰尔总是喜欢规规矩矩地做事情，他从来不会违反大眼的任何规则。

“好的，”我说，“好主意。”于是我转过身去。

“全放进去了。”过了一会儿皮特对我说，于是我转过身来。

“我是大眼。比赛现在开始。安妮，请开始读诗。”

我站起来走向箱子。我把手伸进去，抽出一张纸来。纸上面的字小而整齐。我开始读了起来。

第24页

“安妮的眼睛像湛蓝的海水……”我读道。利奥大笑起来。我停下来，生气地看着他。“不许笑，”我说，“否则我就没法儿读了。”

“是啊，”皮特说，“记得外卖之夜！”

“对不起，”利奥说，仍然微笑着，“我会尽量不笑的。”

奈杰尔满脸通红。我想我知道为什么——他是那种写字又小又整齐的人。我猜这是他的诗。

“我重新读。”我说，然后咳了一声清清嗓子。

“安妮的眼睛像湛蓝的海水；

它们让我期待她能和我约会。

我还没有问过她，所以在那一天到来之前，

我希望我不管怎样她都喜欢。

我想帮她学做饭，

我想教她享受一本好书。

我们迥然不同，但关键是，

我真的很想让她戴上我的戒指。”

诗读到一半时，利奥的肩膀开始晃动起来。他用手捂着嘴巴，但我能看到他笑得眼泪从脸上流了下来。皮特和西蒙也在笑，而奈杰尔看起来简直尴尬极了。

第25页

“这诗，嗯……挺好的。”我说，不知道该说些什么。听到这个，利奥再也忍不住了，他大声地笑了出来。奈杰尔愤怒地站了起来。

“噢，利奥，成熟点！”他大声喊道。

第 3 章　赢家与玩笑

第26页

利奥试图停止大笑，但没有成功。

“这是一首很……不错的诗。”我再次说道，虽然事实上我一点儿也不喜欢它。写诗的人，奈杰尔，似乎对我不满意。他想要大大地改变我，但他仍然说想要我戴上他的戒指。我觉得这点相当难以置信。

奈杰尔仍然愤怒地盯着利奥。“你从来都不认真对待任何事，对吗，利奥?”他说。

利奥笑着说：“我尽量不那样。”

“算了，奈杰尔，”皮特温和地说，“坐下来，好吗?这本来只是为了好玩儿嘛。”

奈杰尔坐了下来，皮特朝我看过来。“也许你应该接着读下一首诗，安妮。”他建议道。

这似乎是个好主意。“好的，”我说，“第二首诗。”我在开始之前又咳了一声。

“她醒来时像只老鼠一样昏昏欲睡，
直到她在咖啡杯中迷醉。
她每天都会出状况，
被路上的东西绊倒。
她说错话还打翻茶杯，
但这个疯狂的女孩儿就是我的真爱。”

第27页

这首诗几乎令所有人都笑了。连我都觉得它很美，并且很像我。从皮特脸上的表情来看，我觉得这是他写的。

“好了，”我说道，从盒子里拿出了另一张纸，“第三首诗。”笔迹看起来既自信又愤怒。我还没有读一个字，就猜到这首诗是西蒙写的。

“不爱运动，

四十岁不到。

不太胖，

幸好是这样！

厨艺糟糕，

脸蛋很漂亮。

她非常风趣，

即使穷得叮当响。

但既然有机会，

何不一起分享？

安，安，安；

我是你的情郎！”

利奥又笑了起来。我不想看西蒙，因为我敢肯定他的表情可以杀人，所以我赶紧继续读下一首。

第28页

“好了，”我说道，“最后一首诗——第四首诗。”这是所有诗中最短的一首。

“她很风趣，她不无聊；

安妮集20位不同的女子于一身。

喜欢大笑，会犯错误，

总是烤煳她的巧克力蛋糕！”

听到这个我们都笑了。前一周皮特过生日，我决定给他做个生日蛋糕。不幸的是，我把它放进烤箱之后就完全忘了。那天天气不错，有点儿热，我们全都待在外面的游泳池里。我们都没有闻到蛋糕的味道，直到它完全被烤焦了。

“我是大眼。所有的诗都读完了。安妮现在要决定哪一首诗最好。获胜者的奖励是和安妮约会。”

“太好了！”有人说道——我想是西蒙。我不确定，因为我正忙着决定我想要谁赢。虽然我理应决定哪一首诗是最好的，但要遵守这个规则很难。我想我知道哪首诗是谁写的，奖励又是跟我约会。我毕竟只是普通人，因此，我正努力决定我想跟谁约会。

第29页

不是奈杰尔，他那些关于戒指和帮助我读书的话已经让我对他失去了兴趣。他难道没想过我读书是为了我的工作吗？至于烹饪，他自己做饭也不怎么样。有一天晚上，他做的咖喱简直辣得没法儿吃。不，不能是奈杰尔，也就是说不能是第一首诗。

利奥？不，那会像是跟我哥哥约会。他的诗显然是第四首，因为它最短，并且利奥那么快就写好了。

那皮特呢，第二首诗？好吧，皮特人挺好的。我妈妈会让我选皮特的，而我确实喜欢他。但事实上，只有一个选择——西蒙，他有着电影明星般英俊的外表。一个有他坐在桌子对面向我微笑的晚上将会非常愉快。所以，就选第三首诗了。

“请安妮说出获胜的是哪首诗。”大眼命令道，我深呼吸了一下。

“诗歌比赛的获胜者是……”我停顿了一下，依次看了每位男士一眼。利奥的脸上还是惯常的微笑，而其他人看起来好像很关心结果的样子。我突然觉得自己很强大。“第三首诗！”

第30页

“耶！”利奥说着，向空中挥舞着双臂。

“什么？”我说。

“我早就告诉过你们了！”奈杰尔生气地站起来说，“我早就说他会赢的。他是个作家！他总会赢的！”

“这一次我同意你的说法，奈杰尔，”西蒙说，看起来不太高兴，“整个比赛简直就是浪费时间。”

我很困惑。我看着利奥。“你写的第三首诗？”我问。他点了点头。

“当然是我写的！”他满脸笑容地说。

“干得好，利奥。”皮特说。他永远是个好人。

“利奥，”大眼说，“你的奖品就是今晚和安妮约会。你们俩必须在八点钟到日记室。其他人应该清楚，今晚不会为他们提供外卖餐了。”

西蒙看起来仍然很不耐烦的样子。“你们知道吗？”他说，“我准备去日记室告诉大眼我对这件事到底是怎么想的。这不公平。”说完他就离开了。

“我要去小睡一会儿，”利奥打着哈欠站起来说，“写诗让我非常疲惫。”

第31页

“把你的西装脱下来，”皮特建议道，“你得打扮得帅气点儿去参加今晚的重要约会。”

利奥点了点头，给了我一个大大的微笑。“好期待啊。”他说道，然后就回了卧室，留下我跟皮特和奈杰尔。

“好了，”皮特说，“我想我最好不要放弃我的工程师工作。我显然不是一个好诗人！”

我看着他。“这些诗都挺好的。”我说。我仍然对不能跟西蒙约会感到失望，特别是他对输了比赛感到非常失望。他显然想赢得与我约会的机会。

皮特大笑。“安妮，如果你那样想的话，我觉得你应该多读一些诗！有谁想喝茶吗？”

“好吧，”奈杰尔难过地说，“我想我不妨来一杯。”

“安妮你呢？”皮特问。

我摇了摇头。“不用了，谢谢，皮特。”我说，心里仍然想着这场比赛。我当时相当确定西蒙写了第三首诗。我浏览了一下那些诗，把第三首诗抽了出来，再一次读了读其中的一部分。

她非常风趣，即使穷得叮当响。但既然有机会，何不一起分享？利奥是什么意思呢？他是在暗示我们为了赢得那一万英镑而谈恋爱吗？嗯，如果是的话，那他就倒霉了！

第32页

“呃……你喜欢我的诗吗，安妮？”奈杰尔问。

我抬头望着他。“哪首诗是你写的？”我问，尽管我知道。

“第一首，”他说，“我自己挺满意的。”而当他微笑的时候，他确实看起来对自己很满意。

突然，我觉得非常生他的气。虽然我没有准备要假装谈一次恋爱来赢钱，但我确实准备捉弄一下奈杰尔。嗯，这样才公平——他不该在他的诗里写那些乱七八糟的东西。

我把诗放下，走过去坐在他身旁。“噢，是的，奈杰尔，”我看着他的眼睛温柔地说，“我喜欢你的诗！你真好心啊，还想着帮我学习新东西！”

奈杰尔的笑意更浓了。“我猜你会喜欢那一部分。”他说，完全没有意识到我对他越来越生气了。

“不过，”我说着向他靠得更近些，把手放到他的胳膊上，“我真正最喜欢的部分是你说要我戴上你的戒指！”

第33页

“哦，那部分啊。”奈杰尔说，开始显得有些怀疑。

“是的！”我说，仍然盯着他的眼睛，“那部分我喜欢得不得了。而且……我的回答是我愿意！”

此刻，奈杰尔的脸色看起来有点儿苍白了。他试图从我身边挪开，但我拉住他的胳膊，又把他拉得更近了一些。“你是什么……什么意思？”他低声问。

“哦，”我解释道，“在那首诗里你向我求婚了，不是吗？而我的回答是我愿意！”

我以前从未见过一个男的看起来如此害怕。他的眼睛瞪得特别大。太好玩儿了。要不是皮特先开始笑起来，我可能还得想办法忍着不爆笑出来。

“你没发现她在开玩笑吗，奈杰尔？”他说，端着茶回来了。

然后我放开奈杰尔的胳膊，哈哈大笑到肚子疼。“你看起来好担心啊！”我终于又可以说话时对他说道。

奈杰尔生气地看着我。“这不好玩儿。”他说。

“噢不，好玩儿。”皮特说，这让我又开始大笑起来。

“如果你不是认真的话，你就不该写进你的诗里。”过了一会儿我对他说。

第34页

“我当时想不到其他的可写啊。”奈杰尔生气地说道。

西蒙从日记室走了出来，他看起来比以往任何时候都更加心烦。“我想告诉他们这不是一场公平的比赛，”他跟我们说，“但他们却什么也不说。”

“那外卖呢？”奈杰尔想要知道。

西蒙摇了摇头说：“这个他们也不肯改变主意。没有外卖。”

“没关系，”皮特说，“来一杯好茶如何？”

西蒙看起来很生气。“这就是你解决所有问题的答案，对吧？”他说，“一杯好茶。不用了，谢谢。”说完，他走出去到了花园里，砰的一声关上了门。

“现在那儿有一个失望的男人。”皮特说。我们全都坐着盯着西蒙离去。

奈杰尔还在生我的气。“他是因为没有外卖失望，而不是因为不能跟安妮约会。”他说道。

“谢谢，奈杰尔。”我说着站起来跟着西蒙走了出去。

西蒙正坐在花园的椅子上。他的太阳镜遮住了眼睛，但是他的嘴巴显示出他有多么心烦。我默默地在他身边坐了一会儿。

第35页

然后我说：“外卖没了我很抱歉。”

他努力挤出一丝微笑。“我烦的不是外卖，”他说，“我只是对被困在这里有点儿厌烦。”

“是吗？”我问。

“是的，”他说，“这和我想象中的不一样。整天坐着无所事事，还有所有这些愚蠢的聊天。有时候这里就像个养老院！我这辈子从来没有这么无聊过。”

“哦。”我说，为西蒙的感受感到失望。

“听我说，你们都是好人，与这个无关，”西蒙继续说道，“特别是你，安妮。只是我是那种需要目标来奋斗的人，而我指的并不是愚蠢的音乐演出或者诗歌比赛。或许最好下一个离开的人是我。"

"哦，"我说道，我说话时脸都红了，"我不希望你离开。"

西蒙冲着我笑了笑。我希望他没有戴着太阳镜，这样我就能看到他的眼睛了。

"没有你的话这里肯定会很无聊的。"我继续说道。

西蒙拉起我的手。我感觉到从他触碰的地方传来一股电流，一直传到我的胳膊上。"你真贴心，安妮，"他说，"别听我乱讲。我只是为自己感到难过。"

第36页

他仍然拉着我的手，这让我觉得勇敢起来。"我很遗憾你没有赢得比赛，"我对他说，"我……我是想让你赢的。"

"啊，"西蒙说，"可怜的安妮。你是不是因为不能跟我约会而感到非常失望？"

我的脸变得更红了。"是的，"我说，"你……你呢？"

西蒙又露出了洁白的牙齿，冲着我微笑。"我当然失望。"他说。他用另一只手触摸我的头发。他的手指修长而自信，非常适合刻胡萝卜花和折纸船。"看看你。"他说。

"怎么了？"我问，抬起一只手来摸自己的头发。我的头发没有全在头顶了——大部分已经垂下来披在了肩膀上。我肯定看起来一团糟。要是我带着梳子就好了。

"搞笑、乱糟糟的安妮，"西蒙轻声说，"要是能跟你约会该有多好啊！不过我们只要另找时间一起做点儿特别的事情就行，对吧？"

紧接着，西蒙决定再去跑会儿步。我看了他一会儿，然后就像做梦般地走回了室内。也许在大眼屋里终究会有一场恋爱——一场我与西蒙之间的恋爱！

第 4 章　凌乱的意大利面

第37页

八点整，我和利奥一起走进日记室。利奥仍然穿着他的西装，看起来还是很帅气。哦，几乎是很帅气——他的领带系得不是很直。至于我，恐怕看起来没有今天早上那么漂亮了。午餐时我们喝的汤，一些汤洒到了我的裙子上。虽然我已经尽力想把它洗掉，但仍然能看到有汤渍。我和汤就是合不来。我当时要是把这条裙子给换掉就好了。

"你认为我们要在日记室里约会吗？"利奥问。我看了看他，一脸惊讶。

"不会吧！"我说，实际上我根本没考虑过这件事。"你觉得不会，对吧？"

"嗯，"利奥说，"约会理应是私密的，不是吗？而只有日记室、洗手间和浴室是私密的地方，对吧？"他笑着对我说："你带香皂了吗？"

"晚上好，安妮。晚上好，利奥。"大眼说道。这次是一个女人的声音。

第38页

"嗨，大眼。"利奥说。

"你好，大眼。"我说，不知为什么我突然感到有点儿紧张。我无法想象为什么——毕竟这只是利奥。如果是我一直期待约会的西蒙，那我就有充分的理由感到紧张了。

"你们今晚的约会将是两人共进晚餐。"大眼告诉我们。我半期待着利奥会开玩笑说在浴室吃晚餐，但他没有。

“如果你们按一下椅子后面墙上的按钮，一扇门会打开，”大眼告诉我们，“进门，你们会看到餐桌在等着你们。”

我和利奥微笑着对视了一下。一扇密门——多么令人兴奋啊！

“谢谢你，大眼。”我说。

利奥已经把手探向椅子后面了。

“找到了！”他说。接着墙上的门开了，他朝着另一边的那个房间走去。“快来，安妮！”他说。我赶紧跟上他。这感觉像是一次真正的冒险。

“噢！”我走进去时说道，“噢！”

房间很漂亮，小小的。墙刷成了粉红色。餐桌上铺着闪着亮光的红色料子做成的漂亮桌布，上面摆放着闪闪发光的银质刀叉。但是我走进去时，让我大吃一惊的是那些灯。目光所及之处它们无处不在——一盏盏小小的银白色的灯，令这房间显得很温馨。真是浪漫无比。

第39页

利奥正为我拉开其中的一把椅子。“请坐。”他微笑着说。

我笑着说：“谢谢你，好心的先生。”

利奥绕到桌子另一头坐了下来。他一坐下，密门就关上了。

“我们被关在里面了。”我说。

利奥抬头看了看墙上的摄像头。“那就只剩下你、我和一两百万的观众了。”他开玩笑道。

“我想知道我们怎么拿到饭菜？”我问。

“问得好。”利奥说。而就在这时，大眼说话了。

“欢迎来到大眼餐厅。”她说。

我的目光与利奥的相遇——他脸上露出了灿烂的笑容——我不得不捂住嘴，以免自己笑出声来。

“你们的第一道菜已经准备好了，”大眼告诉我们，“按一下餐桌下面的按钮，一扇门就会打开。”

“他们很喜欢他们这里的按钮，对吧？”利奥说着弯下腰去找。

第40页

“这次让我来按！”说着我快速弯下腰去餐桌底下找。“在哪儿呢？”我开始在餐桌下面摸索。因为桌布挡着视线，我很难看得见按钮。我撩开桌布，看见利奥在桌子下面对我微笑。

第41页

“你倒过来看很不一样了。”他说。

“你没变，”我笑道，“你看起来还是一样。”

“谢谢！”他说，“我想按钮在那儿。”

我看到了他指着的地方。“哦，是的。”我说完伸手去按下按钮，立刻从上面某处发出了一个声响。我快速抬头想看看发生了什么。不幸的是，我动作有点儿太快了，结果头撞到了餐桌上。

“哎哟！”我说，捂着我的头。

“你没事吧？”利奥问。

“没事，没事。”我不耐烦地说，“看那里！”

一扇小门打开了，墙上出现了一个洞，洞里有两只碗。

“让我来。”利奥说。他今晚显然表现出了最好的一面。他走到墙上的洞口前，端着两碗看起来很好吃的水果回来了。

“我很高兴不是汤。”我说。

利奥笑着说：“大眼不会一天之内两次对你那么不厚道的。”

第42页

“他不会吗？”我说着拿起了一块水果。

“今晚是她。”利奥说。

“哦，对，”我说道。“很抱歉，是她。这到底是什么水果？”我问，“你知道吗？”

“不知道，”利奥说，“不寻常的东西。不过挺好闻的。”

我把水果放进嘴里咬了一口，水果汁立刻沿着我的手臂流了下来。“噢！”我说，而利奥笑了。“为什么这种事情不发生在你身上呢？”我问。

他摇了摇头。“我不知道，安妮，”他说，“这是人生中无法解释的事实之一。安妮·泰勒等同于混乱和事故。”

“我不是完全无可救药的。”我一边说，一边试着用手帕擦掉手臂上的果汁，开始有点儿恼火了。

“当然不是，”利奥同意道，“你不爱运动，不到四十岁，也不太胖……”

“好了，好了，”我打断他，“谢谢你。不管怎样，利奥·布朗等同于什么呢？如果我是混乱和事故，那你是什么？”

“你说呢，”利奥说着咬了一大口水果，“你觉得利奥·布朗等同于什么？”

“开玩笑和睡大觉，”我想都没想就脱口而出，“利奥·布朗等同于开玩笑和睡大觉。”

第43页

“那是在这里，”利奥告诉我，“但这不是真正的利奥·布朗。”

“那‘真正的’利奥·布朗是什么样子呢？”我问道，又试着咬了一口水果。

“嗯，他很爱思考。等思考完之后，他实际上会非常努力地工作，当他不和朋友们见面或社交时。”

“你在这儿也思考很多。”我告诉他。

“是吗?”利奥问。

我点了点头。“是的。嗯，虽然你总瞎聊和开玩笑，但你也会观察我们，而且你很认真地听我们说什么。有时候我觉得我们所有人最后都会成为你其中一本书中的角色。”

利奥摇了摇头。“在来大眼屋之前，我必须承诺不会把这里发生的任何事写进我未来的作品中。这也包括我在这里遇到的任何一个人。所以不用担心，你是安全的。你不会在机场拿起我的一本书，发现我把你写成了杀人犯。”

“我无论如何都不会是一个非常令人信服的杀人犯，”我对他说，“杀人犯可不会犯我犯过的所有错误。”

“你曾经犯过的最严重的错误是什么?”利奥问，“你最尴尬的时刻。”

第44页

我想了想。有太多错误可以拿来说了。“哦，”我说道，“有一次我跳进泳池时，比基尼上衣滑落了下来。还有一次，我还是学生的时候在一家医院实习。我要给卧床的病人发放食物，而我却把一大碗豌豆弄到了地上。豌豆滚到了所有病人的床底下。”

利奥开始大笑。我并不介意，现在回想起来实在是好笑。当时花了好长时间才找回所有的豌豆。

“还有我把两名小学男生锁在了博物馆的一个房间里，那也不是一个很好的时刻。”我继续说道。

“你是故意把他们锁在里面的吗?”利奥问。

“不是！”我不耐烦地说，“当然不是。我不知道他们在里面。他们躲了起来，想跟老师开个玩笑。我以为所有人都从房间里出来了，于是就把门锁上了。那个房间只有博物馆的内部人员带着才能进去。”

“他们整晚都被锁在里面了吗？”利奥想搞明白。

“没有，”我说，“只待了十分钟左右。不过因为我把房间的灯关了，所以里面很黑，而且里面放了一些埃及人的尸体——你知道的，就是木乃伊。”

第45页

利奥大笑着说：“我猜那些男生再也不会跑开躲起来了。”

“他们可能甚至再也不会去参观博物馆了，”我说，“他们真的很害怕。老师也很生气。老板狠狠地批评了我。”

“可怜的安妮。”利奥说。

“我厌倦了人们总是认为我无药可救，”我说，“要是能够被别人认真对待该有多好啊。”

利奥看着我。“你的鼻尖上有果汁。”他说。

我生气地伸手去拿我的——现在已经很湿的——手帕。“你看到没？”我边说边用手帕擦着鼻子，“肯定不能指望有人认真对待我了，对吧？”

墙上的洞里传来一声响动。我跟利奥同时抬头看去，看到的是两大盘非常凌乱的意大利番茄牛肉面。

“哎呀，不！”我说，“我可不会吃意大利面啊！”然后我看了看利奥，我们俩都开始笑起来。

“好吧，”他一边说，一边收拾着我们的水果碗，“我有个建议。”

“什么建议？”我问。

“嗯，”利奥说着走过去取意大利面，“大眼让我们吃意大利面显然是有原因的。”

第46页

“是的，”我说，“是为了让我看起来尽可能愚笨！”

“我建议我们俩都表现得很笨，我们都尽可能地弄成一团糟。我们甚至也不必让衣服保持干净。如果大眼想要一团糟，我们就给她一团糟吧！”

我冲他笑了笑。“你疯了，”我告诉他，“你知道吗？”

“好多前女友都这么对我说过。”他说。他把其中一盘意大利面放在我面前的桌上。“不过我也愿意认为自己很有趣。那你觉得呢？我们要不要做点儿脏乱而有趣的事情？”

反正我吃意大利面肯定是一团糟了，不妨照计划做好了。“那好吧，”我说，“我们就这么干！”

“好，”利奥说着举起了他的叉子，“一、二、三，开始！”

第5章　离别之夜

第47页

晚餐结束时，我的脸上沾满了红色的番茄肉酱，而利奥的头发里也有意大利面，到处都是意大利面。我们一个劲儿地笑，我都累得不行了，仿佛又回到了五岁的感觉。

我冲着桌子对面的利奥笑了笑。“谢谢你。”我说。

“谢我什么？”他问。

“嗯，”我说，“谢谢你让这件事变得有趣。要是跟一个会因为我弄得一团糟而感到尴尬的人一起吃晚饭的话，那太可怕了。”

利奥看着我说："那你觉得其他人中哪一位会觉得尴尬呢？"

我想了想。"可能是奈杰尔。对，肯定是奈杰尔。他会觉得特别尴尬，整顿饭会变得很安静。"

"除了你吃意大利面时发出的声音？"利奥微笑着说。

"是的，"我同意道，"除了那个。"

"你认为还有谁会觉得尴尬？"

第48页

我又想了想。"可能是皮特，"我说，"但他人太好了，所以他不会说出来。"

"讨人喜欢的皮特。"利奥说，而我笑了笑。

"他真的是讨人喜欢的皮特。"我说。

利奥看着我。"那西蒙呢？"他问，"如果皮特是讨人喜欢的皮特，那西蒙呢？"

我用叉子玩着盘子里剩下的意大利面。我认为是性感的西蒙，但我没有那么说。"爱运动的西蒙？"我反而提议道。

"那我呢？"利奥问。

我看着他，考虑了一下。"爱笑的利奥，"我说，"毫无疑问。有时候——尤其是我们需要有人来清洗脏盘子的时候——懒惰的利奥。"

利奥冲着我笑了笑。"别当糟糕的安妮。"他开玩笑道，然后我笑了。

"真好笑。"我说。

突然间利奥的神情变得严肃起来。"你知道西蒙也会因为你吃意大利面的样子而感到尴尬的，是不是？"

我看着他，感到很困惑。"哦，"我说，"我觉得他不会。"

“他当然会。”利奥说。

“他不会的！”我争辩道。

“你只是觉得他很好，所以你不愿意去想他任何不好的地方。”利奥对我说。

第49页

“不对，”我说，“我了解西蒙，仅此而已。他不会那样的。他真的是个好人，而且他喜欢我。”

利奥看起来很生气。“为什么你们女孩子一遇到长得好看的人时总是如此盲目呢？”他问，“任何人都看得出来这个人只对他自己感兴趣！他是个彻头彻尾的自私鬼。”

“西蒙对自己不能参加这次约会感到特别失望！”我生气地说。

“但愿他能这么想，”利奥说，“但这什么也说明不了。这个人冷酷无情，他单薄得像……我不知道怎么说才好，像一张纸一样。”

“西蒙才不是……”我刚开口，利奥就打断了我。

“哦，我不是指身体上单薄。”利奥说，“这个人的身材堪称完美，这是肯定的。令我担忧的是他的头脑——他的头脑和他的心。在我看来，这两样东西他都没有。”

“这个嘛，”我说，“我完全不同意。”

“没关系，”利奥说，“你可以不同意。”他停顿了一下，然后看着我说：“不过我说得没错，你会知道的。”

这次谈话后我们俩之间没那么自在了。当密门再次打开，约会结束时，我感到很欣慰。

第50页

我和利奥走出日记室时，皮特笑了起来。“你们俩进行了一场食物大战吗？”他问。

我抬手摸了摸自己如番茄般通红的脸。我只顾忙着跟利奥生气，完全忘记了乱糟糟的意大利面。

“算是吧。”利奥看着我回答道。

“大眼忘记给你们提供刀叉了吗？”西蒙看着我红红的脸问。

我的脸立刻变得更红了。我避开利奥的眼神说：“我和利奥只是玩了一下。”

“我可不觉得好玩儿，”奈杰尔说，“那些意大利面会弄得浴室一团糟的。”

利奥开始笑起来。“我们拭目以待吧，好吗？”他说完朝浴室走去。

“真没礼貌，”皮特说，“他都不问问你要不要先用浴室，安妮。”

“利奥没有的东西多着呢，”西蒙说，“他没礼貌，他不爱动，他不是个好厨师，他不风趣……”

“哦，西蒙，”皮特说，“这一点我可不同意你。利奥绝对很有趣。”

是的，我想。他很有趣，非常有趣。突然之间，我感到……怎么说呢，有点儿难过。在我跟利奥争吵之前，这是一个非常美好的夜晚。我真希望我们没有争吵过。

第51页

“哦，”西蒙说道，“明天就是‘离别之夜’了——有人要离开了。我们会知道公众的想法，对吧？如果他们和我一样认为利奥不风趣，认为他只是令人讨厌，那他就会离开大眼屋。”

第52页

在“离别之夜”我们总是很紧张，尽管我们所有人都试着用不同方式掩盖这种情绪。西蒙一般会在外面慢跑，直到大眼叫他坐在沙发上。我们必须到沙发那里听取投票结果。其他人会坐在一起笑——通常是笑利奥讲的什么事。我们假装自己毫不在意，而事实上我们所有人都很担忧，没有人想离开大眼屋。

这次的“离别之夜”有所不同。利奥一整天都比往常要安静，而我和他之间的相处仍然有点儿不自在。我觉得奈杰尔看起来仍然很生我的气，所以他没怎么说话。皮特是唯一一个心情不错的人，但甚至连他也没有什么要说的。于是，在等待被告知谁会离开的时候，我们成了非常安静——可能也相当无聊的一群人。

这是一个温暖的夜晚，通往花园的门都开着。每一个“离别之夜”，屋外都会有一大群人。他们来看那个被告知离开大眼屋的人，现场总是很吵。那天晚上的确非常吵。我们能听见人们在大喊大叫，但我们听不清他们在喊些什么。

第53页

坐在沙发上，等着看你是否会被选中离开，这是件非常奇怪的事情。你会想到走出去面对所有那些叫喊着的人，想到所有对着你的摄像头，以及你会被问到的所有问题。等待投票结果就像在等待一场考试的结果一样。

在“离别之夜”，我也常常会想到我的家人、朋友以及屋外的生活。我想念他们，所以每次我没被选中离开时，我都会觉得有点儿伤心。尽管能留下来我也很开心。我想这听起来有点儿疯狂，但很难准确地描述那种感觉是什么样的。

这个“离别之夜”，我试着不去想任何事情。但是很难什么都不想，于是，我就想着那天早上我收到的礼物。是的，又一份礼物——一张用圆形香皂刻出来的笑脸！非常简单，但它让我笑了。

奈杰尔却没有笑。他当时只裹着一块浴巾走进厨房，生气地问："谁把香皂藏起来了？"

所以，我想，不是你给我送的礼物。

那天晚上，我们坐在沙发上等待维奥莱特·卡尔顿跟我们说话时，奈杰尔仍然看起来气鼓鼓的样子。我们都知道她在大眼屋外的人群中。我们随时会知道谁要离开。

第54页

我抬起头，看到西蒙正在看着我。"我希望你不会离开，安妮。"他微笑着说。

"可能是你会离开。"利奥对他说。

"你们俩别再吵了。"皮特开始说，但就在这时，维奥莱特·卡尔顿跟我们说话了。

"大眼屋，"她说，"我是维奥莱特。"外面的人群非常吵。为了让我们听见她的话，维奥莱特几乎是扯着嗓子在喊。"票数已经统计完毕。公众做出了决定。今晚要离开大眼屋的人是……"维奥莱特在告诉我们名字之前总是会停顿一下，这让观看这个电视节目的人更加兴奋。"……奈杰尔！"

我们全都看着奈杰尔。他笑了，但他的脸却红了。

"奈杰尔，"维奥莱特说，"你有五分钟的时间跟大家告别并收拾好你的行李。"

奈杰尔站了起来。我们全都看着他。还没等我们开口，他说道："没关系。我很高兴能离开，我已经受够这个地方了！"说完他就去卧室收拾他的行李去了。五分钟后，他走了。

第55页

“那么，”皮特笑着说，“现在只剩下我们四个了。”

没有人回应。我们只顾着听门打开后奈杰尔走出去时人群的叫喊声了。

第 6 章　食物与跳跃

第56页

“大眼想要你来给剩下的三位男士分配一个任务，安妮。”大眼告诉我。这次是一个男人的声音。“和上次一样，这个任务必须体现出他们对你的感觉。”

大眼召唤我去日记室的时候我正在泳池里，所以现在我是穿着泳装坐着，把椅子都弄湿了。

我不想让男士们再为我做一次任务，可我知道大眼不会改变主意，所以我没有抱怨。相反，我坐在那儿思考自己可以提出什么建议来。

那天早晨，我又收到一份礼物。是一盘水果，可能是摆成了一张脸或其他什么形状。但遗憾的是，我醒来的时候盘子已经摔到了地上，所以，我也不确定。我仍然想知道是谁在给我送礼物。或许我可以选择一个能帮我找出是谁送我礼物的任务。

“好了，”我对大眼说，“我想到了一个任务。”

“你可以告诉我你的想法吗，安妮？”大眼问。

第57页

“我想让他们为我做一样东西，”我说，“我不介意是什么——他们可以做他们所喜欢的东西。但它必须是一份花心思的礼物——他们认为我真的会喜欢的一样东西。”

大眼停顿了一会儿。我等待着，想象着不同的大眼们在讨论我的主意。

“大眼接受你为今天的任务出的主意，安妮，”大眼最后说道，“请你去告诉男士们他们要做什么。他们有两个小时的时间来为你准备礼物。在他们准备礼物的时候，你必须在卧室里等着。”

太好了——独自在卧室里度过无聊的两个小时。不过，要是能找出是谁在送我礼物，那还是值得的。

* * *

“你想让我们做什么样的东西？”在我告诉他们任务之后西蒙想问清楚。

“那由你们来决定，”我告诉他，“大眼希望它是能展示你们对我的感觉的东西。我觉得你们应该努力想想我需要的东西，或者你们知道我会喜欢的东西。”

西蒙和皮特一副若有所思的样子。利奥正微笑着。“你已经有想法了吗？”我问他。

第58页

他的笑容更灿烂了。“或许吧。”他说。

“我是大眼，”大眼说，“今天的任务现在开始。安妮，请回到卧室。”

“祝你们好运！”说完我就走开了，好奇自己的计划能否成功。我真的很想找出是谁给我留的那些礼物。

* * *

一点钟的时候，大眼让我到生活区去。我到那里时，发现只有皮特在。我可以看到其他人在外面的泳池里。利奥看见我后透过窗户跟我挥了挥手。

“发生什么事了?”我问皮特。

他冲着我笑笑说:“大眼让我先给你展示我的礼物。”

我也冲他笑笑,环顾了一下房间。“好,”我说,“在哪里呢?”

“在这儿,”皮特说,“麻烦你来这边好吗?”皮特带着我来到餐桌前,我看见那里有两盘食物在等着我们,盘子非常大。“我决定给你做一顿午餐,”皮特告诉我,“我妈妈总是说,要想抓住一个人的心就要先抓住她/他的胃!”

“是的。”我说,不知道说些什么。说实话,我并不觉得很饿。天气很热,而皮特做了肉、土豆和蔬菜。我更愿意吃份沙拉。“我奶奶也常这么说。”我说。

第59页

“嗯,”皮特说道,脸上仍然带着灿烂的微笑,“希望那是真的!”

我在其中一盘食物前坐下来。皮特真的想要赢得我的心吗?他真的想让我像女朋友一样喜欢他吗?他之前可没有给过我任何暗示。他一直对我很好,但他对每个人都很好。他就像是一个朋友,而不是男朋友。也许他是那种不能轻易表达自己感受的人。

“这看起来……不错,”我拿起刀叉,鼓起勇气说,“你一直很喜欢做饭吗?”

“噢,是的,”皮特说,然后他开始跟我讲起他是怎么学会做饭的,他最喜欢做些什么,他做饭时犯的错误……我听着,一边嚼着东西一边时不时地点点头。每次他停止说话时,我就再问他一个问题,好让他继续说话。我想我是要把他的注意力从我身上转移开,因为我知道自己绝对不想让他把我当成女朋友。我只是对他没有那种感觉,而且我不希望他是那个给我送礼物的人。

在我吃完尽可能多的食物之后——那也只有不到半盘子的东西——我冲着皮特笑了笑。

第60页

“非常感谢你，皮特，”我说，“太好吃了。不过或许我现在得去看看西蒙和利奥给我做了什么。”

“可是用餐还没有结束呢！”皮特一边说一边跳了起来。他走到冰箱那儿拿了两份特别大碗的冰淇淋回来。

等我最后走进花园时，我觉得都有点儿想吐了。

“你好，安妮！”西蒙从泳池里出来说，“准备好接受我的礼物了吗？”

“她看起来好像需要先休息一下。”利奥笑道。

“她当然不需要休息！”西蒙一边说一边用一块毛巾擦干身子。

换作其他任何时候，我一定会很享受地看着西蒙擦干身体，但此刻我不是。“嗯，实际上……”我开始说道，但西蒙已经扔掉毛巾向我走来。

“来吧，”他说着抓起我的胳膊，“我们有事情要做。”

他不是在开玩笑。西蒙给我的礼物是一个体能训练计划。“当然，你并不胖，”他说，“但每个人都需要保持身体健康。只需要跟着我做就可以了。”然后西蒙开始又跳又跑又拉伸。我用尽全力跟着他做，但是天气很热，而且我的胃里塞满了食物。西蒙的每个动作又非常快，他总是在我还没做完拉伸就开始了跳跃，或者我还没完成跳跃他就在拉伸了。

第61页

“对不起，西蒙。”我不停地说。

“没关系，”他说，“你做得很好。”

可是我做得并不好，而利奥明显觉得这一切非常滑稽。他坐在泳池边上微笑着，有一次我真的摔了一跤时，他哈哈大笑起来。我开始真的生起他的气来。西蒙显然也生他的气了，因为他跳着跳着突然停下来，伸手把利奥推到了泳池里。

可是利奥觉得这更加有趣了——当他把头露出水面时仍然在哈哈大笑。

“对你来说什么都是笑话，是吧？”西蒙生气地说。

可是利奥说不出话来，他笑得太厉害了。

我以为西蒙会跳进泳池揍他一顿，但他反而看着我说：“好了，这就是我给你的礼物，安妮。如果你每天都这么做，那你的身体很快就会达到极佳的状态。”

第62页

我累得几乎说不出话来。“哦，”我说，“谢谢你，非常感谢，西蒙。”

“不客气。”西蒙礼貌地说，“好了，安妮，如果你不介意的话，我现在要进去冲个澡。如果我再待在这儿的话，我可能会做出什么事来让利奥永远闭嘴。”

我看着他走开，然后在花园里的一把椅子上坐下来。利奥还在笑。

“闭嘴，利奥！”我闭着眼睛说道。

我听到他走过来在我旁边的椅子上坐下。“对不起，”他说，“可是你不知道那有多好笑！”

“哦，”我有气无力地说道，“我想我知道。如果你的礼物跟食物或身体锻炼有关的话，那你还是别跟我提了！”

“我的礼物是关于改善你的心智的。”他告诉我。

“改善我的心智？”我疲惫地重复道，“你能为我做出什么来？”

“我给你做了一份调查问卷，”利奥说，“一份让你思考并回答的问题清单。”

我看着他。“关于什么的问题？”我问道。

利奥微笑着说：“关于你。”

“我？”我问。

他点点头。“是的，”他说，“设计它们的目的是让你思考你想从生活中得到什么，以及现在的你到底有多快乐。”

第63页

“那你觉得这份问卷是我想要的，是吗？”我问。

“你说过这礼物必须是你喜欢的或者我们认为你会需要的某样东西。”他提醒我道。

我受够了。皮特以为我需要食物，西蒙以为我需要健身，而现在利奥以为我需要改善心智。似乎没有人对现在的我感到满意。而我仍然不知道是谁在给我送礼物。

“那继续吧，”我不高兴地对利奥说，“给我看看你的这份问卷，我会尽量回答你的问题。”

第 7 章　问题，问题

第64页

最后，利奥把问题读给我听。

“好了，”他说，“问题一。如果你只能再活一年，你会做什么？”

“这个问题很难回答啊！”我说。

"它们都很难回答。"利奥高兴地告诉我。

"噢，我不知道，"我说，"放弃我的工作？周游世界？除非它真的发生了，不然有谁知道他们会做什么？"

"问题二，"利奥继续说道，"你认为在你死之前哪三件事是你必须做的？"

"所有的问题都是关于死亡的吗？"我问他。

"不，不全是。"他说，"说吧，三件事。"

"好吧，"我说，"我想想。"实际上，这个问题并不难回答。我只是觉得跟所有人分享自己的隐私有点儿傻。"我会周游世界，我会跟我的意中人生个孩子，还有我会买套房子。"

第65页

"按这个顺序吗？"利奥问。

"这个嘛，"我说道，"我想最好是先有房子后有孩子。"

"而且得先有意中人再有小孩儿吧？"利奥开玩笑道。

"真好笑。"我说，"来，下一题。"

利奥低头看了看他手中的纸。"好的，"他说，"现在我们来谈谈你的工作。问题三是你工作中最糟糕的事情是什么，问题四是你工作中最好的事情是什么？"

"哦，"我说道，"我想最糟糕的是它每天都差不多，每周都是一成不变的日常工作。而最好的事情……"我顿了一下，意识到我的老板有可能正在看这个节目。或者，如果他没在看，那在博物馆工作的其他人可能正在看。

"快点儿啊，"利奥说，"说实话。"

"好吧，"我说，"我想我工作中最好的事情就是每个月月底我都能拿到工资。"我看着利奥。"这不算很好的回答，对吧？"

"哦，"利奥说道，"这刚好把我们引入到问题五——如果你梦想的工作是环游世界，拍摄并书写美好的事物与地方，那你为什么不这么做呢？"

第66页

"我想是因为我负担不起，"我说，"或者我只是不够勇敢或不够有志气迈出第一步。我不知道。"

利奥看了看我。我期待着他对我的答案说些什么，但他没有。"好了，问题六，"他反而说道，"你打算何时去上摄影课？"

我去年就计划开始上这门课，前年也是，但我没去。"我希望是在秋天吧。"我说，"说真的，利奥，你知道你的这份问卷弄得我有多烦吗？我感觉自己像个彻头彻尾的失败者。"

利奥看起来并不在意。"这全是为了你好。"他对我说道，"好了，最后一个问题。"他停顿了一下，看着我。

现在我开始有些恼他了。为什么他会觉得他有责任让我思考所有这些事情呢？好吧，我可能的确需要考虑一下；不，我绝对需要考虑一下了。我正处在人生的十字路口，需要做一些决定。但我不需要在上百万电视观众面前这么做。

"你觉得什么样的男人才是你完美的男朋友？"

第67页

我笑了。不用再想我的工作问题实在是太好了。"噢，"我说，"这很简单。我完美的男朋友会是一个善良的人，一个享受生活但真正在乎他自己所做的事情的人，一个喜欢跟我做同样事情的人。"

"所以，"利奥问，"他不必长得很好看？"

"嗯……"我说，"是的，但得让我觉得他很迷人。"

利奥大笑。我看着他说："我不觉得这有什么好笑的。"

"是不好笑，"他说，"你只是很诚实。"

"你希望我诚实作答，不是吗？"我说，"不管怎样，我敢肯定你没有和你不觉得迷人的女生交往过吧？"

"当然没有。"利奥说。

"那不就得了！"我说。

"但她们也并不都完美，"利奥说，"有时我觉得某个人的笑声迷人，或者她们微笑的样子，她们热爱生活的方式。只是必须得有某种东西迷人，就是这样。"

我生气地看着利奥。"先是职业建议，现在是恋爱建议，而你还是单身，对吧？"

第68页

"是的。"利奥说。

"而且你单身有一段时间了吧？"

"是的。"利奥说。

"所以你也并不是什么都懂，对吧？"我问，"不然的话，你现在早就不是单身了。"

"我从来没说过我什么都懂啊。"利奥说。

我看着他。"你总是强辩到底，对吧？"我说，"你一定要在争论中获胜才行。"

"我们是在争论吗？"利奥问。

我的头开始疼起来。"走开，利奥。"我说着闭上了双眼。

耳边传来纸张翻动的声音。"我本来就要走了。"利奥说。

"很好。"我说道。而当我再次睁开眼睛时，只有我一个人了，问卷放在了我旁边的椅子上。

我立刻为自己对利奥发脾气而感到内疚。他的问题令我感到不舒服，这并不是他的错。我感到不舒服是因为我对自己当下的生活不是完全满意，而他的问题让我想起了这一点。我感到被困住了，但又好像对此无能为力。这就是为什么我想要参加这个节目——为了做点儿什么，什么都行，不一样就行。而这的确是不一样。

第69页

“嗨。”听到这和善的声音我抬起头笑了起来。皮特正站在我旁边。“介意我过来吗？如果你宁愿一个人待着，尽管说。”

我的确想要一个人待着，可我不能这么说。皮特只是想表现得友好，我不想像伤害利奥那样伤害他。“不介意，”我说，“没关系。”

“一天下来你是不是觉得累了？”他问。

我笑了。“是啊！”我说，“当然累啦。我头疼，两条腿也疼。”

“那你的胃呢？”皮特问。

“哦，”我说，“到明天为止我不想再吃任何东西了！我已经很饱了。”

皮特笑起来。“对不起，”他说，“我做的饭实在太多了，对吧？”

“差不多够六个人吃了。”我说。

“我来自一个大家庭，”皮特告诉我，“我习惯了做大餐。”

“皮特，这顿饭挺好的。”我对他说，“作为礼物，它是一个很好的想法。”

我笑了，我们一言不发地坐了一会儿。有只鸟在什么地方唱歌。四周很宁静，我觉得自己开始放松下来，于是我闭上双眼晒会儿太阳。

“我想知道下一项任务是什么。”皮特说。

第70页

“我不想考虑这事儿！”我说道，仍然闭着眼睛。

“明天晚上这里就只剩下三个人了。”皮特说。

“噢，对，”我说，“我都忘了，明天又是一个‘离别之夜’。”

“是的，”皮特说，“不过我们都在这里待不了多久了，很快我们全都会回到自己的正常生活中去。”

我不想回到自己的正常生活。利奥的问题让我意识到我对所有的一切是多么不满意。问题是：对此我该怎么办？

“嗯，”我说道，尽量让自己看起来开心些，“我希望离开的不是你。”

皮特看着我。“真的？”他说，“你宁愿是其他人中的一个离开？”

我睁开双眼，思考着这个问题。我绝对不希望离开的人是西蒙。而至于利奥……我不确定。他会令我觉得疲惫，但我真的希望他离开吗？事实上，出于某种奇怪的原因，我并不想他走。

我冲着皮特笑了笑说：“我不希望你们任何一个人离开。”

“我们中必须有一个人离开。”他说。

第71页

“这倒是真的，”我同意道。我看着他，又一次觉得他真是个好人。“你真的很喜欢自己的工作，对吧？”我问。

“做工程师吗？”皮特说，“是的，我热爱它。”

“你最喜欢它的什么地方？”我问道，想起了利奥的问卷。

皮特并不需要多想。“我喜欢完工之后看到自己帮忙造出来的东西，”他告诉我，“一座桥或一栋楼房——你站在那儿看着它，心想，这是我参与建造的。这感觉很棒。”

“肯定的。”我说道。

我们沉默了一会儿。我想象着皮特站在那儿望着他建的其中一栋楼房，脸上露出灿烂的笑容。如今在看着一群小学生离开博物馆后，我显然从来没有像他那样笑过。我想我刚开始工作时才有过。

“那你从来不会对建桥感到厌倦吗？”我问皮特。

“不会，”他说，“每座桥都是不一样的。”

“真棒，”我说，“你非常幸运。”

皮特停顿了一会儿，然后他问：“等这一切都结束之后，你愿意来看看我建的其中一座桥吗？”

“我愿意……”我开口说道，但是接着我转过头来看着他的脸。他看着我的样子让我感到有些后悔自己回答得太快。

第72页

皮特伸出手来摸着我的头发。突然，他的脸似乎离我的脸很近了。“我希望这一切结束之后我们能共度一段时光，安妮，”他说，“很多时光……”

皮特情绪的变化让我大吃一惊。正当我努力想着说些什么的时候，他的脸靠得越来越近了。他要亲我了！

我一跃而起。“抱歉，皮特！”我迅速说道，“我得去……去……去一下洗手间。”然后我跑进了屋里。

第8章 吻

第73页

“大眼屋，我是维奥莱特，”维奥莱特·卡尔顿在第二天晚上对我们说道，“今晚要离开大眼屋的人是……”

在另一张沙发上，皮特躲避着我的眼神。他白天大部分时间都是那样。我们俩都没提起在花园里发生的事情。利奥和西蒙一直在周围，所以我和皮特没有独处的机会。不过那天早上，我去洗手间的时候，我们迎面相遇了。

“皮特，”我当时说道，“关于昨天的事……”

“忘了它吧，”他快速地对我说，“我真是太傻了，居然以为你会有兴趣做我的女朋友。”说完他就走了，留下我在那儿想着这件事是不是应该怪我。我想我并没有做什么事情让皮特认为我觉得他很迷人。我是告诉过他我希望他不会离开，但我只是随便说说而已。噢天哪，或许这真的是我的错。

“……皮特。”维奥莱特·卡尔顿说出了结果。

第74页

“早猜到了。”皮特说，然后站起身来。利奥和西蒙走过去跟他握手。我也站了起来，但我没有走过去。我不确定皮特是否希望我过去。皮特要离开，我很难过。他是一个很好的人，虽然我不想让他做我的男朋友，但我确实喜欢他。

“真不走运。”利奥说。

“没关系，”皮特说，“下一个肯定会是我。你们俩都是强劲、有魅力的人——不到最后是不会被淘汰的。”

“那我呢？”我说道，皮特终于向我看过来。

“噢，不会的，安妮，”他说，“不可能是你。观众想要把你留下来，他们想看浪漫的爱情。”他向我走来并抓住我的胳膊，低下头看着我的脸。“而且不管怎么样，你漂亮、风趣、充满爱心……”他停下来冲我笑了笑。“还有很多优点。任何一个真正跟你谈恋爱的人都会是个非常幸运的人——无论是在这里还是在外面。”当我忙着仔细琢磨这些话时，皮特吻了我。

五分钟之后，他收拾好行李，正等着门打开。

“皮特，”维奥莱特·卡尔顿说，“你现在必须离开大眼屋了。”

第75页

一道道的门开始打开。皮特拎起包，然后严肃地看了看西蒙和利奥。“你们最好对安妮好一点儿，”他对他们说，“我会看着你们的。”

然后，他走过那些门，门随后关上了。西蒙、利奥和我站在那儿，等着这栋楼外面的门打开时会传来的尖叫声和呐喊声。在出口外面有台阶——当你离开大眼屋时要走上台阶，然后其他门会打开让你出去。

突然，等在外面的人们的喧闹声响了起来——那声音像一堵厚厚的声墙。不管我听过多少次，它总是让我感到意外。

“再见，皮特。”我轻轻地说道。

我旁边的利奥打了个哈欠，伸了个大大的懒腰。“‘离别之夜’令我感到好累，”他说，“我想我该休息一下了。”说完他就走了，剩下我和西蒙单独一起。

西蒙在其中一张沙发上坐下来，我走过去跟他坐在一起。“那个家伙需要去看医生。”他说。

我看着他问道：“谁？皮特吗？”

“不，是利奥，”西蒙说，“他总是需要睡觉。不过现在想想，皮特可能也应该去看医生。很明显他病得很严重，非常严重的相思病。”

第76页

“别说了，”我说，“我感觉好像是我做错了什么似的。不过我不认为自己做了什么事情让他相信我对他有感觉，但我还是觉得内疚。”

“不用内疚，”西蒙建议道，“你长得漂亮，风趣又体贴，这又不是你能控制的，对吧？人们爱上你并不是你的错。”他看着我，握住了我的手。“顺便说一下，他说的那些话都是对的。”

我突然感到一阵燥热，低下头看着被他握住的手。“哦，”我说，“你真的这么认为吗？”

“是的，”西蒙说，“我确实这么想。不过我觉得他列的清单里还落了一样重要的东西。你还相当性感，尤其是脸上沾着意大利肉酱的时候。”

我抬头看着他说：“你是在笑话我。”

西蒙笑了笑。“只有一点点，”他说，“那只是因为我喜欢你。在大眼屋里的所有女生中，你是留下来的最后一位，我为此感到非常非常高兴。”

我不知道该说什么，一时间我既开心又觉得不好意思。“你真好，西蒙。”我说。

“我这么说不是为了讨好你，”西蒙对我说，“我这么说是因为我就是这么觉得的。”

我不知道该说什么。西蒙之前从来没有这么关注过我。他坐得离我这么近，并直视着我的眼睛，这弄得我很紧张。他是一个很有魅力的男人，我感觉到了他离我这么近的效果，有点儿像被火车撞了一下的感觉。

第77页

“哦……谢谢你。”我紧张地说道，看着他的嘴巴，想知道他会不会在数百万观众面前吻我。皮特吻了我，这是事实，但那不一样。那是一个告别之吻，而这个会是……嗯，说实话，我不确定。一个

“你好”之吻？一场恋爱的开始？

沉默的气氛持续着，事实上这一刻可能就那么几秒。但是坐在那儿，西蒙低下头那样看着我，感觉像是过了好几年。我必须说些什么，做些什么，否则我的心跳要停止了。

我张开口说话，不知道自己要说什么。“我……我觉得，我们……我们最好开始做晚饭。”我说。

西蒙看着我。显然这不是他期待听到的话。“有趣的小安妮，”他温柔地笑道，“在这种时候还想着食物。”

我们身后某处有一扇门打开了。“有人提到食物了吗？”利奥扯着响亮的嗓门儿问，“我好饿。安妮，你准备做什么吃的？”

第78页

* * *

“你今晚感觉如何，安妮？”

我已经在日记室待了大约20分钟，我来是想自己一个人待会儿。我知道这可能听起来很疯狂，但是我要避开的是西蒙和利奥，不是大眼或看节目的人们。假如利奥没有跑进生活区谈论晚餐和肚子饿的话，会发生什么事情呢？西蒙会吻我吗？我想让他吻我吗？从我第一次见到西蒙的那一刻起，我就很喜欢他。我当然想让他吻我，难道不是吗？

“我感到……很困惑。”我告诉大眼。

“为什么呢，安妮？”大眼问道。那天晚上的大眼是个女的。“我不确定自己对任何事情的想法，”我对她说，“我脑子里一片混乱。”我感到有点儿难过，我能从我的声音中听出来。“我意识到自己对大眼屋外面的生活并不满意，但我不知道该怎么办。我感觉还没有准备好离开这里。这听起来是不是很愚蠢？”

“你觉得听起来愚蠢吗，安妮？”大眼问道。我忘了大眼从来不会说出自己的想法。

第79页

“是的，有点儿，”我说，“但我控制不了，这就是我的感觉。而西蒙和利奥一直在那儿争吵，对我一点儿帮助都没有。”

“你觉得他们为什么争吵呢，安妮？”大眼问。

“我想是因为他们不是一类人吧，”我说，“而且他们俩都是那种自以为是的人。”

接下来大眼又停顿了一下。我想知道西蒙和利奥是不是还在争吵。我想知道他们俩有没有人去做晚饭，很可能没有。这一点西蒙和利奥倒是很相似——他们似乎都认为做饭是女人的事情。

“你发现是谁在给你送礼物了吗，安妮？”大眼问。

“没有，”我说，“还没发现。但如果明天早上没有礼物的话，那我就知道是皮特了。不过我不认为是皮特。其实，我正想着今晚整晚都不睡呢。我想我可能会当场抓住留礼物的人。”

“那如果你真的发现了他们，你会问他们什么？”大眼问。

“我想我会问他们为什么这么做，”我说，“我的意思是，这只是个游戏吗？还是因为他们在意我才送礼物的？”

第80页

“你想过要问问是谁在给你留礼物吗？”大眼问。

我摇了摇头。“我不好意思问，”我说，“我不知道为什么。我更愿意当场抓住他们。”

又是一阵沉默。我想象着自己躺在黑暗中等待着西蒙或利奥给我送礼物。我得在上床之前喝些非常浓的咖啡，这样才能保持清醒。

“你希望送你礼物的人是谁，安妮？”大眼问。

这是我不希望她问我的问题，这是目前最困扰我的问题。“我不知道。”我说。

在大眼说话之前又是一阵沉默。我选择不去打破这沉默。“大眼祝你好运，安妮。”她终于说道。

我挤出一丝微笑说：“谢谢你。在最后的‘离别之夜’之前，我还需要想好另一个任务吗？”

“大眼已经选好明晚的任务了，”大眼告诉我，“明天下午你们全都会收到任务指令。”

第81页

“我等不及了。”我说道，这不完全是实话。我从椅子上半站起来。“对了，”我说，“我最好去解决一下今晚的晚餐。谢谢你的倾听，大眼。”

“你随时都可以跟大眼交谈，安妮。”大眼提醒我道。

“谢谢。”我对她说，接着就离开了。

令我吃惊的是，在我离开日记室时，西蒙正在厨房里做饭。利奥像往常一样坐在沙发上，看上去陷入了沉思中。我想知道他是不是在想他的下一个故事。

“晚餐很快就好了，安妮。”西蒙微笑着对我说。

“太好了，”我说，“闻起来好香。需要我来摆放餐具吗？”

“好的，麻烦了。”西蒙说道。

我走到放刀叉的抽屉那里拿出来一些。西蒙看了过来。“我们只需要两副刀叉。”他说。

我没明白他的意思。“什么意思？”我问。

“我们只需要两副刀叉，”西蒙对我说，“我只做了足够我和你吃的饭。”

“哦。”我惊讶地说。

房间那头，利奥看起来不只是惊讶。“你没做足够的食物给我吗？”他问。

第82页

“没有，”西蒙不高兴地说，“我没做。在你赢了那场愚蠢的诗歌比赛的时候，我承诺过安妮我们会一起做些特别的事情。这就是我们的‘特别的事情’。你可以自己做饭啊。”

“你为什么不早点儿告诉我？”利奥生气地说道。

“你没问啊，”西蒙说，“你知道的，这里不是餐厅！”

又一次争吵！也许这一切终将结束也不是件坏事。

“我相信这些够我们所有人吃了，”我说，“我不需要吃很多。”

但是西蒙并不打算改变主意。我正在观望时，他端着一个深平底锅来到桌子旁，开始把食物盛到两个盘子里。“来吧，安妮，”他说，“把刀叉拿过来。我们别让它凉了。”

于是，两天之内，我第二次坐下来享用一个男人专门为我准备的饭菜。我现在明白了皮特当时是想用食物来向我表达他的情感。西蒙也是这样想的吗？

用餐之后会发生什么呢？

但是，用餐之后什么都没有发生。也不可能发生什么，因为利奥没有让我和西蒙独处。在我们吃饭的时候，利奥一边做着他的三明治，一边大声地唱着歌。他还把三明治拿到餐桌上吃。

第83页

当西蒙给我们俩煮了咖啡并建议到花园里喝的时候，利奥很快端着自己的咖啡跟了出来并坐在我们旁边。

“你介意吗？”西蒙生气地对他说道。

“毫不介意！”利奥高兴地说。

“我是说，你介意走开吗？我和安妮需要些私人空间。”

“实际上，”我说，“我正打算进去再煮点儿咖啡。”

西蒙一脸惊讶地问：“你已经喝完那杯了吗？”

我一直记着我整晚不睡觉的计划。“是啊。”我说，“你们俩谁还要再来一杯吗？”

“不用了，谢谢。”西蒙说。

“那好吧，”利奥说，“安妮，你真是太好了，主动给我们煮咖啡。”

我刚回到屋里，就听见他们俩又开始争吵起来。他们就像小孩子一样。

我端着咖啡出来时，利奥喝了一口便拉长了脸。“这么浓！”他说，“你是想让我俩整晚都睡不着觉还是怎样啊？”

第84页

我没有回答。紧接着，利奥便被叫到日记室去了。

“终于只剩我们俩了！”西蒙说着把他的椅子拉得离我更近了，然后伸手把我的咖啡杯拿开。

这一次西蒙没有给我机会去谈论食物，甚至没有给我思考的机会。他立刻开始吻我。那是一个很甜蜜的吻，感觉真的很好。尽管我很喜欢，但恐怕我心里同时又感到极其尴尬，因为有数百万观众在观看我和西蒙亲吻。我妈妈在看着我和西蒙接吻！不过我非常希望贾宁和格洛丽亚在看，特别是贾宁，她一定嫉妒得要命！

最后，西蒙抽开身低头看着我。“可爱的小安妮。”他柔声说道。

我以为他要再次吻我，但正在这时，利奥回来了。

“哦，对不起，”他说，“我打断什么了吗？”

没等西蒙回答，我就站了起来。不知什么原因，我特别想要逃离。“其实，”我说，“我正准备去睡觉。明天早上见。”

我的确上床去了，虽然我一点儿也不累。我想这一方面是因为我喝了浓咖啡，另一方面是因为我没法儿不去想西蒙吻我这事。我喜欢西蒙很久了。他一直对我很友好，但之前他从来没有表现出想要和我有超越普通朋友的关系。他对我的感情好像发生了变化。这令我很困惑。

第85页

大概一小时之后，其他人都回来上床休息了。我仍然想要找出是谁给我留了那些礼物。明天是最后一天了，所以，如果到明天早上我还没有找到答案，我可能永远都找不到了。我通过想博物馆的事情让自己保持清醒。我想了一个游戏玩儿，想象着博物馆里的每个房间和那里面所有的东西。如果我犯了错误或忘记了什么，我必须重新开始。博物馆里有很多东西，所以这让我的脑子停不下来。可是随着时间的流逝，要保持清醒变得越来越难。

当有东西把我吵醒时，我才意识到自己睡着了。有人起床了。我躺着一动不动，等着那个人走过来到我的床前留下礼物。但他没有走过来；相反，他离开了房间。两分钟之后，他回来又躺回床上，我才意识到他肯定只是去了一趟洗手间。

接下来我知道的就是，所有灯都亮了，我独自一人在房间里。现在是早上了，从周围的东西判断，我睡过头了。我很生自己的气，低头看着自己的床，想看看那里有没有什么东西。床上有东西。我捡起来看了看。是一把钥匙，一把用纸剪出来的钥匙。钥匙。多么奇怪的礼物啊。什么意思呢？谁留下的？西蒙还是利奥？我到底能找出是谁吗？

第 9 章　真相之舞

第87页

星期六——在大眼屋内的最后一天——是漫长的一天。自从那个吻之后，我觉得在西蒙身边待着很奇怪。我不确定要跟他说些什么。我不知道那个吻意味着什么，我感到很困惑。不过反正我也没有单独跟他在一起过。利奥一直在那儿。我想我们都不敢相信这是我们在大眼屋内的最后一天了。

终于，下午的时候，大眼把西蒙叫到日记室里，给他下达最后一项任务的指示。

“好了，”他出来时对我和利奥说，“最后的任务是一场我与利奥之间的跳舞比赛。”

“你是说你跟我必须一起跳舞吗？”利奥问。

西蒙看起来很生气。“当然不是！我们俩都要跟安妮跳舞。她跟我学探戈，跟你学牛仔舞。”

我立刻担忧起来。“等一下，”我说，“我舞跳得可不怎么样。我学不会跳探戈和牛仔舞！”

第88页

西蒙冲我笑了笑。“你跟我一起跳会没事的，”他说，“我跳得很好。”他又低头看着他的那张纸。“我和利奥每人有一个小时的时间跟你练习，然后真正的比赛在晚上七点钟开始。”

“但我们怎么学那些舞蹈呢？”我问，“你知道怎么跳探戈吗？”

“不知道，”西蒙说，“但大眼已经为我们准备了这两种舞蹈的跳法说明。我相信不难学。”

“嗯，我也不会跳牛仔舞。”利奥说，“你猜怎么着？我敢说它非常难学。我对跳舞一窍不通。”

“哎呀，”西蒙不友好地笑着说，“听到这个我好难过。来吧，安妮，我们最好现在就开始。”没等我回答，西蒙就站起来朝厨房区走去。“这里的地板非常适合跳舞。”

我慢慢站起来。我不想跳舞。我知道自己会在数百万观众面前出丑，再一次出丑。我说自己跳舞不好，那是实话，西蒙自己很快就会发现这一事实。

第89页

“不要让他把你指挥得团团转。”利奥建议我道。

我不想对他笑，因为西蒙看起来很生气。“安妮会玩得很开心的。”他说。

“那是第一道命令，安妮。”利奥对我说。

“我建议你研究一下自己的舞蹈说明，利奥。”西蒙说完转过身去背对他，低下头看他自己那份说明书了。

在等待的时候，我努力回想自己对探戈的了解。我知道它起源于阿根廷，有点儿像戏剧。我之前在电视上看过别人跳探戈，但从来没想过自己会去跳。

“好了，”几分钟后西蒙对我说，“跳探戈时，男女双方要挺直身躯，动作迅速而突然。”西蒙挺直后背给我做示范。“这是关于性的舞蹈。”他身后的利奥笑了起来，但是西蒙假装没听见。“有时它甚至可能与谋杀有关。”他继续说，“一直以来它都是一种关于烈火与狂热的舞蹈。但最重要的是，无论男方还是女方，跳的时候都坚决不能笑。他们必须一直保持严肃的表情。”

第90页

在我们学跳探戈的时候，这对我来说是最难的事情。噢，舞步已经够难了——我跳得一点儿都不好。但在保持严肃方面我真的是无能为力。

“这不好笑，安妮，”西蒙一次又一次地对我说，“我不明白你为什么总是笑。”

“对不起，”我说，“可能是因为我紧张。我紧张的时候总是会笑。”

“哦，请你再努力一点儿吧。”他说。

我努力了，但是没有用。当西蒙看着我，好像他不确定是要吻我还是要杀了我时，我又情不自禁地笑了起来。

西蒙很生气。“你确定你在努力吗，安妮？”他问。

“是啊，”我对他说，“我真的在努力。”

“好吧，再努力一些。”他说，“我告诉过你：这种舞是关于性与谋杀的，是很严肃的。”

我确实努力了，非常努力。但是我只顾忍着不要笑出来，结果把舞步全弄错了。

“不对！”西蒙说，他此时已经明显对我很厌烦了，“不是那样，像这样！我想我们刚学过这部分！”

“对不起，”我再次道歉，接二连三地道歉。快到一个小时了，我迫切需要休息一下，但是西蒙还想继续练习。

第91页

“我需要坐下来，西蒙。我的脚很疼。”我试着对他说，但他不听。

“马上就好，”他一直说，“我们再复习一下最后那部分。”

我不知道这样持续了多久，但利奥突然又出现了，他走了过来。“我想你的时间到了。”他一边对西蒙说，一边领着我走向沙发。

“坐在这里吧，安妮，”他说，“把脚抬起来。”等我把鞋子从我那可怜的、疼痛的双脚上脱下来之后，我照他说的做了。

我沉默了一会儿。我在忙着思考。跟西蒙的舞蹈练习真的很不愉快。西蒙好像并不在乎我累不累。他只是不停地跳啊跳啊，告诉我该做什么，在我出错时他就抱怨。我之前从未这么想过，但西蒙有点儿像我的老板——彭福思先生。他指望我工作很长时间，又不给额外的工资。

“我还得和你一起学牛仔舞呢。”我最后对利奥说。

“没关系的，”利奥说，“我们会补上的。”

我猜他只是好心，因为他知道我累了，可我突然生起他的气来。“难道你不想赢吗？”我问他。

第92页

我突然意识到自己经常生利奥的气。我想那是因为我希望他……怎么说呢，更多地去争取。他真的看起来对任何事情都不怎么在意。但他肯定在意自己的写作，因为他在这方面很成功。如果他不在意的话他就不会成功了。

“有那边那位‘完美先生’在，我永远赢不了舞蹈比赛。”他说。

“你有可能赢的，”我说着站了起来，“别那么悲观。来吧，你至少要尝试一下吧。”

“哦，那好吧。”他说。

于是，我们开始练习起来，这与跟西蒙一起跳时截然不同。跟西蒙跳的时候一直好严肃，我总是害怕跳错了。可跟利奥跳就完全不一样了。我们总是跳错，但我们都一笑置之。

“对不起！”每当利奥踩到我的脚时他就说。

“别那么快！”我喊道，因为他带着我们一起转圈转得太快了，感觉整个房间都开始转起来了。

作为舞者，我们简直糟糕透了，但是很好玩儿。自从上次的意大利面晚餐之后，我就没这么开心过了。

但最终练习时间结束了，我们不得不为真正的比赛做好准备。七点钟，比赛按照大眼的安排开始了。我们又一次要穿他们给的服装。我的裙子是黑色的，有宽大的裙摆，我移动的时候它就绕着我的腿舞动。我很喜欢。西蒙穿的是一条黑色紧身裤，配一件黑色紧身衬衣，看起来无比帅气。利奥……哦，利奥穿的是一件粉色的紧身衬衣，搭配一条粉色的紧身裤，看起来……好傻，真的很傻。西蒙经常做各种运动，很注意自己的身材。但是利奥又高又瘦，还有点儿肚腩。粉色配在他身上一点儿也不好看，他自己也知道这一点。

第93页

我尽力不笑出来，但就是忍不住。西蒙也笑了。“你看起来就像生活在地底下的某种动物，”他不客气地对利奥说道，“你看上去就像一条蚯蚓，一条蚯蚓！”

我望着利奥的脸。有那么一瞬间他看起来很受伤，但随后他笑了起来。“哦，好吧，”他说，“我倒是一直都很喜欢蚯蚓的。”

“我也是。”我说。那不是实话，但我只想对利奥说点儿好听的。我突然意识到自己有多么喜欢他。噢，他惹我生气，我希望他能更积极一点儿，但我真的喜欢他。突然，我意识到我想让他赢得这场舞蹈比赛，而不是西蒙。不幸的是，我知道那不太可能。

“舞蹈比赛现在开始，”大眼对我们说，“安妮将先跟西蒙跳探戈。”

第94页

西蒙站起来等着我过去和他跳。他用胳膊搂着我，我们等着音乐开始时，我抬头看着他的脸。我不知道自己期待着要看到什么，但我所看到的不是我所期待的。西蒙面无表情，就像一块木头。

这次跟西蒙跳探戈时我一次也没笑，跳完后他对我非常满意。

“太棒了，安妮！”他最后对我说道，“我这次赢定了！”

“我们就尽情享受吧。”轮到要跳牛仔舞时利奥对我说。于是我们就按照他说的做了。我们一阵乱跳，哈哈大笑；我们甚至加了一些舞蹈说明中没有的自编舞步。那好玩儿极了，但那不是他们让利奥跳的舞蹈。我知道他将几乎毫无悬念地输掉这场舞蹈比赛。

我们仨都坐在沙发上等着大眼来跟我们说话。

“我是大眼，”大眼说，“舞蹈比赛的结果将由公众投票决定。今晚九点我们会告诉你们获胜者是谁。”大眼再次开口之前又停顿了一会儿，然后，他所说的话令我们全都惊讶得面面相觑：“输了比赛的人今晚将离开大眼屋。”

第 10 章　赢家与输家

第96页

我们都无法相信自己的耳朵。

“这不公平，”西蒙说，“不过，我还是会赢的。公众显然看得出我跳得比你好，利奥。”

利奥只是看着他。

“那样的话，安妮，就只剩下我和你了。”西蒙朝我这边微笑着说道。

我突然觉得自己一点儿也不喜欢这个想法。哦，西蒙确实长得好看，他的吻技也确实不错。但我忍不住想起他对利奥的舞蹈服说过的难听的话，还有我们学跳探戈时他对我指手画脚的样子。假如大眼屋内就剩我俩了，我不确定自己能想出什么话跟他说。

九点钟之前的时间过得非常缓慢。然后，维奥莱特·卡尔顿终于跟我们说话了。

“大眼屋，我是维奥莱特，”她说，“票数已经统计出来了。输掉舞蹈比赛并且要离开大眼屋的下一位是……”

第97页

西蒙在沙发上正襟危坐。利奥半躺着，双手交叉放在脑后。我不耐烦地上下抖动着脚。等待的时刻好像持续了很久很久。

“……西蒙！”维奥莱特终于说完了。

维奥莱特说话的时候我正看着西蒙的脸，所以我看到他听见自己的名字时脸色变得通红。

“西蒙，”维奥莱特继续说道，“你有五分钟的时间收拾行李并道别。”

我站起来向他走过去。“噢，西蒙，”我说，“我很遗憾。”

“是啊，”利奥说，“你绝对是跳得最好的。我很遗憾。”

西蒙看着他。“你一点儿都不遗憾，”他冷冰冰地说，“我们俩从一开始就互相讨厌。我觉得没必要因为我要离开了你就假装喜欢我。”

利奥点点头说：“有道理。”

西蒙站起身来。“如果你们想听真话的话，我迫不及待要离开这里了。”他说，“还有，你们知道吗？我不在乎是否还会再次见到你们中的任何一个。”说完他就朝卧室走去。

第98页

我盯着他的背影，无法相信自己刚刚听到的话。如果西蒙这样想的话，那么那个吻是怎么回事？我跟在他后面走过去。

“由他去吧，安妮，”利奥劝我，“他明显是个输不起的人。”

“不，”我边说边继续走着，“我想要一个解释。”

在卧室里，西蒙正往行李箱里扔衣服。我走进房间时他头也没抬。

“你是在假装，对吗？”我说道，“假装喜欢我。”

“不完全是，”西蒙说，听起来有点儿厌烦，“我没有不喜欢你。说实话，在所有其他女生都离开之前，我根本没怎么关注过你。之后，怎么说呢，我想八万英镑总比七万英镑好得多。”

“所以你就设法利用我！”我愤怒地说，“非常感谢！”

西蒙合上行李箱，把它从床上拎起来。他终于看我了。“给你一个建议，安妮，”他说，“如果你不想听到答案，就不要问问题。”然后他走了出去。

两分钟之后，他离开了大眼屋——还有我的生活——永远地离开了。这样就只剩下我和利奥两个人了。

第99页

“你没事吧？”利奥正坐在一张沙发上，而我坐在另一张上。我们仍然能听见外面人群的呼喊声。西蒙离开大眼屋时，他们真的很疯狂。

我和利奥坐得相隔甚远，但又足够近到让我意识到他在担心我。

“是的，”我说，“我没事。”我确实没事。或许西蒙曾试图利用我，但这并不重要。我没有真正受到伤害，因为我现在知道自己对他并没有太深的感情。

一旦我开始把西蒙跟我的老板彭福思先生作比较，我就停不下来了。西蒙总是认为他什么都是对的，跟彭福思先生一样。西蒙只在对他自己有利时才对我好，这也跟彭福思先生一模一样，比如，当他想要我周末加班的时候。

我真的喜欢过西蒙，但现在我明白自己对西蒙的真实面目一点儿也不了解。我只看到了他好看的外表，仅此而已。但我开始明白，好看的外表并没有那么重要。你是什么样的人才重要。

第100页

“你在意大利面晚餐时说的关于西蒙的话，”我现在对利奥说道，“你说得没错。”

利奥笑着说：“啊，意大利面晚餐。那是个美好的夜晚。”

我回想起利奥头发上的意大利面，自己也笑了。“是啊，”我同意道，“的确是。”我看着他。“你是怎么看出西蒙的真实面目的？”

“在文学界有很多跟西蒙相似的人，”他对我说，“当你处在顶峰、成功的时候，他们喜欢你。但如果你的下一本书失败了，他们就不想再认识你了。”

“虚假的朋友。”我说。他点了点头。

“是啊，”他同意道，“不过说实话，我也很嫉妒西蒙。他充满魅力又自信满满，而女人总是更喜欢像他那样的男人。”他自嘲了一下。“我跟女人相处就像我跳舞一样没用，所以我当了一名作家。写东西很简单。你可以让侦探抓住凶手，或者让男生得到女生的芳心。现实就难多了。”

我看着他，意识到了什么。“你对什么事情都能开玩笑，”我对他说，“为什么这么做呢？”

“我想是为了避免受到伤害吧。”利奥回答道。

“那管用吗？”我问。

第101页

“嗯，我觉得管用，”利奥说，“因为这样能阻止人们接近我。不过最近我慢慢懂得了避免与人亲近并不总是件好事。”

这是我跟利奥之间最严肃的一次对话。我想问问他是什么意思，但大眼打断了我们的谈话。“我是大眼。公众现在开始投票决定大眼比赛的获胜者。结果将在十五分钟后公布。”

我和利奥互相看了看彼此。十五分钟，十五分钟。无论我是否赢得比赛，我很快就要回归自己正常的生活了。我可能再也见不到利奥了。突然之间我感到特别难过。

“好吧，”利奥说，“快要结束了。”

“是啊，”我说，“要结束了，我……我感到伤心。”

我想再和利奥聊一个晚上——最后一个机会去了解这个躲在玩笑背后的真实的男人。

我想第二天早上醒来看看是否有人给我留了礼物。因为如果我醒来时发现有礼物，那一定就是利奥送的了。我突然意识到自己真的、真的希望是利奥一直在给我送礼物。我非常喜欢利奥。我们一直相处融洽，只是我把那些感觉误以为是单纯的友谊了。我和利奥是朋友，但对我来说却不仅如此。

第102页

“要结束了我也感到难过，”利奥静静地对我说道，我突然想不到要跟他说些什么。现在我终于意识到自己对利奥的感觉了，我感到害羞。

我告诉自己，只剩下几分钟了，现在说点儿什么，否则就来不及了。

但是已经来不及了。

“大眼屋，我是维奥莱特。”维奥莱特·卡尔顿说道。

是结果，出来了。

我和利奥互相看了看。我想走过去坐在他的身边——去握着他的手或者做点儿别的什么——但是我太害羞，不敢这么做。

“票数已经统计完毕，现在我可以告诉你们大眼比赛的获胜者是……”维奥莱特像往常一样停顿了一下。这次沉默似乎持续了很久。然后，维奥莱特终于又开口了：“……利奥！”

我跳了起来。“噢，利奥！”我说，“祝贺你！”我太为他感到开心了。我跑到他身边，想要亲吻他或者拥抱他，但利奥只是呆呆地坐在那儿。他看起来好像不敢相信这件事。

“安妮，”维奥莱特继续说道，“你已经输掉大眼比赛，现在必须离开大眼屋了。你有五分钟的时间收拾行李和道别。我会来接你。”

第103页

“我……我得去收拾东西了。”我对利奥说。利奥没回答，我梦游般地走回了卧室。利奥赢了，不是我，可是我不在乎。我没有赢得七万英镑，但我也不在乎。我从未期待过要赢。不过现在我要走上屋子的那些台阶去面对人群了。维奥莱特会在电视上采访我。不过，最糟糕的是，我还没告诉利奥我对他的感觉。也许我应该现在告诉他，在我离开之前。

可是当我走回生活区时，利奥仍然坐在我离开前他所在的位置。

他看起来不像赢了大奖的人。

“我无法相信，”他对我说，“肯定是弄错了。”

“不会错的，”我说，“你听到维奥莱特说的了。你赢了。”

“但是为什么呢？”他说，“他们为什么会投票给我？”

我知道这可能是说出我的感觉的唯一一次机会了。“因为你风趣，”我说，“还很善良。”

“不，我不是这样的人。”利奥说。

我冲他笑笑说：“好吧，你可以是的。在我们吃意大利面的那次约会中，你对我很好。只要你想，你就可以让别人非常快乐。”你令我快乐，我本想补充一句，但又一次为时已晚。

第104页

“大眼屋，”维奥莱特说，“我是维奥莱特。安妮，你现在必须离开大眼屋了。”

一道道门开始打开。利奥站起来。“我不明白你为什么没有赢。”他对我说。

“不，”我对他说，“公众的选择很明智。”

“安妮，请离开大眼屋。”维奥莱特说。

我拎起我的包。“再见，利奥。”我说。

“好吧，”他说，“出去见。”

我点点头，然后穿过那些门。它们很快就在我身后关上了。我紧张地走上台阶。当我走到最上面时，通往外面的门打开了，而当我穿过门去时，一阵嘈杂声扑面而来。

“安妮！安妮！”人群呼喊着，“安妮！我们爱你！”

之前在我的人生中还从未发生过这种事情，而且我知道这种事情不会再次发生在我的身上。我感觉……自己像个电影明星。

维奥莱特就在那儿，她伸手过来给我一个吻。

“安妮！”她说，“对着镜头笑一个！”我的确笑了，成百上千的摄影师给我拍照，夜空都被照亮了。

第105页

我和维奥莱特穿过叫喊的人群，我不知道自己想笑还是想哭。如果他们对我这个输掉比赛的人都这样，那对赢了比赛的利奥会是什么样？

利奥。此时此刻他感觉如何？

我很快就知道了。我和维奥莱特坐在电视摄像机前的椅子上。在那儿，在一个非常大的电视机屏幕上，是利奥。他仍然穿着那身粉色衣服，独自坐在大眼屋里。他双手捂着脸，看起来……很孤单。

“可怜的利奥，”维奥莱特说，“你看他！你才离开五分钟，他就已经想你想疯了！”

“他无法相信自己赢了。”我说，但维奥莱特摇了摇头。

“不，那不是他的问题所在，安妮。”维奥莱特说，“他在想你。我知道，全国人民知道，等你看完这个，你也会知道的。”

维奥莱特指了指电视机。画面从独自坐在大眼屋生活区的利奥切换了。有很多关于利奥的镜头剪辑，讲述着他在大眼屋内生活时发生的故事。但每一个画面也跟我有关。

第106页

有我和利奥一起玩意大利面并哈哈大笑的画面，有利奥问我问卷上的问题的画面，有我和利奥一边乱跳牛仔舞一边欢笑的画面。很多事情我已经知道了。但还有其他一些事情，一些我不知道的事情。当西蒙告诉我该做什么时，利奥看起来很生气的画面；西蒙吻我时利奥在生活区嫉妒地注视着我们的画面；还有利奥在日记室里的画面。

“我忍不住去想她，”他告诉大眼，“她风趣、聪明……还漂亮，只是她自己不知道而已。她总是说自己多么无可救药。其实我们在很多方面很相似，但我觉得她还没有意识到。”

“你会告诉安妮你对她的感觉吗，利奥？”大眼问。

“有什么用呢？只要‘完美先生’还在这儿，她连看都不会看我一眼的。”利奥笑着说，“我以前从没谈过恋爱。这感觉真的很伤人，不是吗？然而，这段经历将对我的创作非常有用。”

最后还有一段用特殊摄像机在夜里拍摄的画面。利奥在我的床上放了一只纸船、胡萝卜花、香皂、脸型的水果、纸钥匙。每次他站着低头看我时……嗯，都充满爱意。

第107页

录像放完了。维奥莱特看着我，而我发现自己已经泪流满面了。

“太甜蜜了，”维奥莱特说，“这个男人从第一天开始就为你疯狂了。安妮，看完这个，你感觉怎样？”

“难过，”我说，“高兴。我……我也不知道。我只是希望他说些什么，而不是浪费了这么多时间。我完全不知道他对我的感觉。”

“如果你现在能跟他说话，你会对他说些什么？”维奥莱特问。

我想都没想，说：“我会告诉他我爱他。”

这正是人群想要听到的回答。我一说出口，他们便发出巨大的欢呼声。维奥莱特满脸笑容。“好了，”她说，“我觉得该是你说这话的时候了。我要跟大眼屋通话。”

“大眼屋，”她说，“我是维奥莱特。”

电视上，利奥抬起了头。

“利奥，”维奥莱特说，“安妮有话要对你说。”然后她看着我，点了点头。

我看着电视上的利奥。他正好也看着我，感觉就像他能看见我一样。在最后一刻，我改变了我要说的话。“利奥，”我说，“你为什么给我做那把钥匙？它有什么寓意吗？”

第108页

自从得知自己赢得比赛以来，利奥第一次露出了笑容。“哦，”他说，“这取决于你想要它有什么寓意。它可能只是一把开启激动人心的新职业的钥匙，或者……它可能代表完全不一样的东西。”

这感觉不像是上百万人在听我们交谈，倒像是只有我和利奥。“比如呢？”我问。

利奥看起来很紧张。“比如……打开我的心扉的钥匙，”他柔声说道，“打开我的心和我的爱。”

他说的时候没开玩笑，也没大笑。我于是知道他决定要赌一把，给某人——我——接近他的机会。

“那要看你更喜欢哪一个，”他说，“选择权在你。”

假若他能看到我的话，就会知道我高兴得哭了。这是一份如此强烈的情感，我觉得自己要爆炸了。“那么，”我泪流满面地说，“我选择心，心和爱情，毫无疑问。”我说完后又哭又笑，坐在那儿看着利奥脸上最灿烂的笑容。演播室里的每个人也都哭了，连维奥莱特也哭了。

第109页

“大眼屋，”她用颤抖的声音说，“我是维奥莱特。利奥，你赢了大眼比赛。做好准备，我们要来接你了！”

然后，她牵起我的手，我们穿过尖叫的人群跑了回去。

“安妮和利奥！”他们喊得声音那么大，把我的耳朵都震疼了。“安妮和利奥！”

接着，大眼屋的门打开了。他站在那里，比赛的获胜者，张开双臂迎接我。当我奔向他的怀里时，我知道自己跟他一样是个大赢家。